"LETTERS TO CHARLES"

Volume 1

Cordial Letters
To and From
An Atheist Friend

By Jomo K. Johnson

Library of Congress Cataloging-in-Publication Data

Johnson, Jomo K., 1980 –

Letters to charles : volume 1 : cordial letters to and from an atheist / J.J. K. Johnson

ISBN 800035-327922

I. Religion. 2. Philosophy.

3. Fiction-Literature

00001423

Letters to Charles

What do dear friends who grew up together do when one abandons his faith in God and turns to atheism? They do the obvious. They remain friends! This witty, funny, and intellectual dialogue follows two young men as they discuss issues such as God, science, ultimate reality, and *Jon & Kate Plus 8*.

Charles is the bright university student who has chosen to cast off the restraints of religion for free thought, skepticism, and naturalist philosophy. J.J., his dear and beloved friend, has just enrolled in seminary to study for the ministry. When J.J. hears of Charles surprising conversion to atheism, the two begin a series of unique correspondence that will challenge both men intellectually. The reader who peers into this authentic conversation will encounter one of the most creative and unique debates on theism and atheism ever seen.

Also included are three apologetical appendixes: Letters of Van Til To C.S. Lewis, Paul Meets Mohammed, and The Last Sinner. Each one of these unique works will aid and add to the reader's experience of being entertained and enlightened by this unique work of Christian Apologetics.

Dedicated to Dr. Scott Oliphant and Dr. William Edgar of Westminster Seminary

Two stalwart soldiers in the defense of the Christian Faith.

Special consideration and thanks is given to Tim Kao of Westminster's Theological Writing Center, and Emily Rubottom (also of Westminster Seminary), for their diligent work in editing this volume. Their help was essential in making this book succinct and concise in all that I sought to communicate.

CONTENTS

PREFACE

What was I to do? In December of 2009, being a new pilgrim to Philadelphia, I was now experiencing the torridness of twenty-eight inches of winter snow in a period of one week. All the northerners were reciting the same hideous mantra to me, "*You know, it usually never snows like this here.*" "*Oh,*" I thought. "*I guess you'll tell me that next year when Hades actually does freeze over.*"

Being confined to the dorm room of the wonderful Westminster Seminary, I attempted to escape the cabin fever by doing one of the things that I love most; writing. I had just finished taking Dr. Scott Oliphint's class: *Introduction to Apologetics*. I learned all the terms as they related to Presuppositional Apologetics. I had been taught the Transcendental Argument for the existence of God, which shows that all logic, morals, and science ultimately must borrow its epistemological capital from the Christian worldview and that God's absolute nature is the only source of logic and morals. I was discipled on the use of logical deduction and the *reductio ad absurdum* (AKA: The "how to make your opponent look like he's wearing invisible pants" argument). And finally, the great warrior apologist himself, Cornelius Van Til was presented in all his glory and grandeur as we were assigned to read, *The Defense of the Faith*. I truly was challenged, engaged, and enlightened by the material presented in the course.

While this class did much to help my understanding of the error of absolute reliance upon the classical method and showed me a new and even better way to engage my opponent, I still leaned toward the Cumulative Case method myself. In comparison with the Presuppositional approach, the Cumulative Case method seeks to persuade and not prove. Adherents to this method include the likes of Paul Feinberg, C.S. Lewis, and Richard Swinburne. This method is a colloquial argument that seeks to extract data and information from all sources, whether they be science or aesthetics, literature or history, philosophy or mythology, in order to *persuade an individual* that Christ is indeed God in human flesh.

I must confess before many witnesses, that when it comes to apologetics, I find myself in a strait. In my heart of hearts, I lean toward the Cumulative Case method, which reveals that even the sublime symphony of sound as orchestrated by Beethoven is only an echo of the universal chord of Deity that holds all life together. Yet, with my utter devotion to Westminster Theological Seminary and the Reformed tradition, my mind also desires to fully embrace the methods of the masters such as Cornelius Van Til, Greg Bahnsen, and John Frame. With the Cumulative Case method, I prove nothing yet demonstrate everything, and with the Presuppositional approach, I can prove that my opponent is a fool. (This is very tempting for an *already-but-not-yet* sanctified man like myself.) I was torn between two lovers. In one (the cumulative), I find beauty and in the other (the presuppositional), I find duty. I quote the great Apostle Paul in stating, "*Oh wretched man that I am! who shall deliver me…*" (Rom. 7:24)

The work you now read, *Letters to Charles,* is the culmination of that struggle. As I recalled and recorded my conversations with an atheist fully engaged in proving his worldview, I began to write this book. It was a challenge to be committed to one systematic method of apologetics, when my opponent was not committed to one systematic method of unbelief. Therefore, I sought the full arsenal of presuppositional, classical, evidential, and cumulative methods to get him out of his bunker of unbelief, so that I might penetrate his pulmonary valve with the sword of the Spirit. Admittedly, at the end of the day, it was the Cumulative Case method that dominated the majority of my arguments.

Did I win the debate? I will let the reader decide. But what I will say was that through the writing of this book and through wresting with the arguments for atheism, I grew as an apologist and a soul winner. The goal for any Christian apologist should never be just to win an argument. It should be to win a soul for Christ. R.W. Dale said that D.L. Moody was the only man he ever heard who had the right to preach on hell, because Moody could not preach it without shedding tears. Knowing the great cost of our testimony, may we Christian apologists also shed tears over those who know not the truth.

Jomo K. Johnson

LETTERS TO CHARLES

Dear J.J.,

I don't have much time to talk now. I've got class in less than a nanosecond. But yes, the rumors are true. I've become an atheist. Deal with it!

Sincerely in Love,

Charles

Dear Charles,

I must confess that your last letter left me quite dumbfounded. Since we are childhood friends and were catechized together in the church, I am quite curious about your current confession of atheism. It seems to me that that school of yours is teaching you some very strange things, or should I say, teaching you *nothing*. You know that I am only a first-year seminarian seeking to educate myself in the mysteries of the Christian faith. Knowing you as I do, I find it difficult to accept that you truly believe the things you say. For how can you truly believe such a thing as atheism? You are basically saying that you believe that no God exists. Well, if you believe that he does not exist why do you first presuppose that he does? This is quite strange, I must say. In any case, I will do my best with support of the Holy Writ to address some of the common atheistic arguments.

I assume that you believe in the Big Bang theory, evolution, and natural selection. Well alright, you have that prerogative. However, those views do not seem to line up with who you are. And when I say "who you are," I don't mean your character, upbringing, or background; I mean who you are as a rational and reasonable man. If you say that random chaos has given life to all things we know, then the products look nothing like the source. What I mean is this: if random chaos is your Father/Your Maker/Your Begetter, then how is it that you stand before me as an rational being? Your words are not chaotic. (Though they are sometimes foolish, they are still intelligible.) The way you walk and move shows order and fluidity. The very makeup of your body and more specifically, your circulatory system, are evidence of a uniquely designed working organism. What I'm saying is that your very physical body provides no evidence for random chaos. I mean, Charles, it should have some indication of that, if spontaneous human combustion was indeed the means of human procreation, but, of course, it is not.

I hope we can talk more about this. But I must go now. Please convert soon.

Your Dear Friend,

J.J.

Dear Charles,

I recall in one of your previous letters, you did not respond to the topic that I discussed. If chaos were the maker of us all, how come we don't look like it? I would assume that the reason you did not broach this subject is that you are searching to find some type of evidence to counteract my statements. Feel free to search as you may; just don't use Dawkins in your defense. His writings, though they at times make for good humor, are a bit of a snooze.

You now bring up of the matter of good and evil. Believe me; I will be brief on this topic because it has already received so much attention. You ask, "How can evil exist if a supposedly omnipotent good God also exists?" This is quite an elementary question, even for you (just kidding , my friend). Well, I assume we are presupposing that God is all-powerful as the Christians say. I would say this in reply: if God does not exist, we have no right to call evil "evil" or good "good." Whatever happens is only "natural." So, what I read on the front page of the newspaper today about the Nigerian man who hid explosives in his underpants and attempted to blow up a plane—this can only be "natural." The same goes for the case of a woman is bound and hidden by her father to be repeatedly raped over a period of years. We can say these things are "natural." Why call these tragic, evil, or bad? We cannot call anything evil or good because what happens is the result of the natural process of natural selection.

You see, Charles, to call something good or evil is to presuppose some standard of morality. And by definition, morality is a system of laws. And a system of laws must presuppose a system- or a law-giver. It seems that we do agree on something after all.

I'm sorry; I have to be on my way. I've got class in 10 minutes. It is Systematic Theology. You probably wouldn't enjoy that class. I look forward to talking to you again soon.

With much sincerity,

J.J.

Dear J.J.,

Hello, dear friend and saint. (I do confess that I consider you a saint, as your and my former faith prescribes, always causes me to smile a bit.) Do you remember that night with me, you and… Ha! (Just in case someone ever reads these letters, I won't go there!).

First, to be an atheist is not to believe that there is no god, but to assert that we have no reasons to believe that he/she/it exists. In the same manner that most people are a-fairian, a-unicornian, a-yetian, etc. The difference? Well, it's simply that in the absence of any evidence supporting a particular claim, we cannot claim with absolute certainty that something does not exist. This does not, however, mean that the claim is thereby endowed with intellectual dignity. On the contrary, in the absence of evidence for god, any discussion about such a being is equivalent to a discussion concerning the color of a mermaid's hair or the length of a unicorn's horn—a pointless discussion.

Secondly, to claim that our origins are due to random chance in the traditional sense of the word is to mislead yourself and your audience. The evidence is that we exist by chance (technically, this is no different from the theistic world view) and that our origins are random in the sense that they have no ultimate plan or purpose.

Nevertheless, the beauty of our universe is that our existence is not the result of random chance, but the result of a series of discoverable intriguing events, with each dependent on those preceding it and all playing out on the stage of a universe far stranger than we can imagine.

Does science have all the answers? No, of course not. By its very definition, science cannot have all answers, but it constitutes the only real and reliable means to any reasonable conceptions about our universe, while attaining a notion of real truth within the confines of human understanding.

This is in stark contrast to the brazen Bronze Age claim to know all things and all purposes for all beings at all times, the pompous, self-righteous claim to have divine authority based on a dusty old book, in which hares chew their cud, women are inferior, and we are all the eternal subjects of an eternal dictator.

As for the question of morality, "we" are the system and "we" are the law- giver and "we" have been changing our notion of morality for as long as "we" have been around. Thankfully, quite independently from the Bronze Age, morality has been reduced to writing in monotheistic teachings.

Believe me, dear friend; we'll be discussing this more.

Charles

Dear Charles,

Hello, friend. How are you doing today? I hope that the spring at XYZ University has brought you warm weather, good friendships, and great food. By the way, I am look forward to seeing how your relationship with the exchange student goes. Here's a hint, don't *ever* let her know the real you. Only a true friend would tell you that.

I see your questions keep coming. I guess you are waiting until I answer enough of them before you write me back a dissertation of why I and the other 5.3 billion people on earth who believe in a God are wrong. Well, I'll be looking in the mail for anything that weighs over a pound. I'm sure any such paper you write would make good kitty litter. By the way, my cat loves the Christopher Hitchens book you sent me for my birthday. Please send more! (Cat litter is getting expensive in this economy.)

I see in your last letter you brought up the issue of the first cause. You quoted Bertrand Russell. I don't know much about Bertrand Russell, but I will say if he is half the philosopher as he is an atheist apologist that my cat would love him, too. I believe he says, "If everything must have a cause, then God must have a cause. If there can be anything without a cause, it may just as well be the world as God." Well, please remember I'm just a first-year seminary student, so my answers might seem simple. I believe when or if a theist says that everything has a first cause we are excluding God himself. We consider God a person and not a thing.

Secondly, if there is no first cause, then time itself would become the first cause. Because whatever was made that was made had to exist in time. And if whatever made what was made was making it for an infinite regression, that would mean that time itself was, dare we say, eternal? Therefore, it would be only right to crown time as the God of the universe. I do agree with this: Something or Someone that is eternal can only be the first cause. Thankfully, that is one of the attributes of the Christian God.

Yours Truly,

J.J.

P.S. Even if time were eternal, mustn't someone first set the clock?

Dear J.J.,

You stated in your first letter, "... Random Chaos has given life..." No one in science treats the Big Bang, abiogenesis, or evolution that way. Physics has a general set of laws that govern the universe. We have observed these laws for centuries now in the natural world. When we expand the scale of these laws we can apply them to the universe. When we see the Doppler effect, we can measure distances and relate them to time. Given the time frames, we can hypothesize causation and then observe the world either refuting or verifying our predictions. The expansion of matter appears to be random, but there are governing forces such as gravity pulling the smaller objects together. Given time, order is created, without a creator, through the laws of physics. If you were to refute that order is not being created, I point you back to the frequency of craters over time. No one in science calls this random chaos. It is a singularity subject to laws.

Abiogenesis is the theory of how life was formed from chemical compounds into RNA. Again, given billions of years, we have a planet with super hot lava, super cold, darkness, light, hundreds of chemical compounds, thousands of combinations of those compounds, and ocean vents that create currents to heat and cool the compounds, until they form a lipid layer and begin to self replicate. At this point, we move into evolution. Again, rather than random chaos, it was chance plus time. And 4.5 billion years is quite a long while.

Evolution is clearly not random chaos. There are chance mutations that are governed by the environment. Simply put, if a mutation gives a reproductive advantage that allows for more offspring, then that mutation will be selected. The environment and competition, rather than chaos or a designer, determine the course of development.

In the same way, morality is governed. If you have a psychopathic killer as a member of your society, then they will wipe out their reproductive ability, thereby ending their chances of continuing on in the gene pool. If they control society through violence and power, eventually society will have had enough of it and overpower them. The Bolsheviks or Louis XV can attest to this. I apologize for my good and evil argument. I was trying to appeal to your worldview. I really don't believe in good and evil nor in the Christian God, for he has changed his mind with the New Testament. It was clearly his own admission that his early years were evil. So much for the never changing laws of morality. Feel free to wear a cotton-wool blend if you like. Hilarious!

So you see how natural laws and time account for everything from singularity to morality. I'm sorry that no one has shown you the bigger picture. I just wanted to show my dear friend how joyous a life can be when it's seen through cause and effect. I no longer have to struggle with the why's of life. I can see it and change my path rather than being subjugated to accepting a predetermined fate from a God who changed his mind after saying that my life was predetermined. If you find joy in not having choice and in being told who to be, then I still accept you as my friend and hope that you have the best life possible. As for me, I'm back to my studies and to convincing my girlfriend that I'm worth keeping around. We enjoy our evenings by quoting Thomas Paine and laughing at Ron Hubbard's *Dianetics.*

With Great Respect,

Charles

Dear Charles,

Well, hello to you, friend. I am glad that in the midst of your business and busyness you have taken time to write your old friend. Tell me again your girlfriend's name. Is it Mary? You know Mary in Hebrew means "bitter." I dare say that her name has fulfilled a prophecy now that she is dating you. Oh, I'm just kidding.

I thank you so much for you last reply and those quality scientific terms that you taught me. Abiogenesis? That must be the book before Genesis of my Old Testament. But listen, it seems to me that you hint but still do not address my issue from my third letter wherein I stated, "if there is no first cause, then time itself would become the first cause. Because whatever was made that was made had to exist in time. And if whatever made what was made was making it for an infinite regression, that would mean that time itself was, dare we say, eternal?" So, when you say that chance + 4.5 billion years equals enough time for RNA to self replicate, I'm thinking... do you hear yourself, man?

Answer me this riddle, chum: "Which came first, time or chance?" It's kind of like asking whether the song or the dance came first. If you say *chance,* then you mean *nothing* came first. So from nihilo comes *something*? And if you say *time,* then it proves my point that you believe time is eternal and therefore my first point is confirmed. (Or maybe you believe that matter is eternal.)

Next, on this issue of morality, you stated in your letter that morality is governed. Governed by whom? Please don't assert that morality is a system of laws instituted by man! For even the most primitive heathen have codes of ethics very similar to the last six of the Ten Commandments. Could it be that there is ingrained in the consciousness of man a moral law? I believe that is what my Bible says (cf. Romans 2:13-15). And I do understand that it is always a temptation to inject Christian interpretation into the argument when you state, the Christian God "has changed his mind with the New Testament. It was clearly an admission that his early years were evil. So much for the never changing laws of morality." I must object by stating that it is impossible for an atheist to understand Biblical Theology unless he is taught. Any time an atheist attempts to do theology its like Edward Scissorhands trying to give you a manicure. The result is always bad.

But as always, I am glad that we can have these discussions. Please know that you are dear to me as a brother, and I long for the chance (did I say chance?), the opportunity to see you again.

Truly Yours,

J.J.

P.S. When are you coming to visit?

Dear J.J.,

It's always great to hear from you. Mary sends her love sans the bitter. She's so good to me and for me. Making time to share our thoughts is very important to me. I look forward to the days when I am finished here at the University so that we can sit down to a cup of coffee and enjoy a lively discussion. I apologize for neglecting your third letter and the discussion of first cause. Let me do so here.

I must say that I've been dancing around philosophically in regards to first cause. Under conventional definitions, it is certainly a quandary. But if I'm direct in regards to the claims made in the Bible, I can address the problem. The Bible spends much of the Old Testament laying out prophecies and generations to fulfill the prophecy from Adam to David and eventually Jesus. James Ussher took much trouble in calculating these generations back to 4004 B.C. Even if he were off by 50%, the last Ice Age never happened, and we need a new explanation for Loch Ness, Sedona, Chinese writing systems, agriculture, etc. So, you see, the claims of the Bible are invalid in the first place. Therefore, it matters not what claims follow. This is why I didn't address your issue of time.

You are not speaking of a Christian God. His time line is laid out, and if you were to use "the length of days" discussion, you would have to explain how plants survived prior to light being in the expanse of the sky between days 2 and 3, not to mention how this light from 13.7 billion years ago reached Earth in 6000 years.

When we attended church together as children, I was taught the Bible by the same teachers that you had. It's interesting how when I sought to further my education away from these teachers, it became clear that those who taught us as children were incorrect, even though my new teachers weren't even seeking to address religion. Let's consider the course on law that I had once.

They taught that in America, I may have any God. That's quite unlike the First Amendment. I learned that it is legal to work on Sundays or Saturdays as I paid my way through school. When I told my parents that I was no longer a Christian, it dishonored them, but no one took me to jail. I certainly waited for it, too. Recently, when Mary cheated on me I went to the cops to tell them, but no one arrived to arrest her either. Then the other day I saw this gorgeous house and I wanted to own it so badly. So I decided to start my own business, and when I told the State Secretary why, I was nervous that my coveting would send me to jail. But, alas, it didn't. I had always heard the propaganda that the Ten Commandments were the source of American law, but why devout Christians would make it a priority to violate the First Commandment with the First Amendment is certainly odd.

I again don't seek to change you. You ask such deep and important questions, and I just want you to have all of the tools. You know how asking too many questions was discouraged. I think that it's because our parents didn't know the answers. The funny thing is, they just taught us what they knew. I know that now my parents ask me questions all the time. I can answer them, and I'll never ask them to stop asking. I find that an intriguing point.

C'est la vie. And so goes the circle and purpose of life. I know more than my parents and hence have a better chance of educating my offspring. It's really a beautiful purpose: to spend your life making a better life for your children. It's quite moving to be an atheist. I hope that God shows you your purpose soon! I'm excited to know what it is.

Enjoy the day, and I can't wait to read your new book. Please let me know when it comes out. I want to be first in line to purchase it. If you have any questions that I can help with, I'll be eager to find the time for you again! Give my love to your parents!

Regards,

Charles

Dear Charles,

Hello friend and fellow townsman. So you're still dating Mary? Man, the females of XYZ University must suffer from extreme glaucoma and cataracts of the retina. You never were a comely man. Ah, I'm just telling you the truth that you already know!

May I just say a quick word from your last letter on the Ten Commandments? Do you not remember the three types of Mosaic laws we learned in our Old Testament class? They are the ceremonial, civil, and moral laws. When the atheists quote an ancient ceremonial law about not wearing two types of garments together, it shows ignorance of Biblical Theology. Their lack of theological knowledge is again apparent, when they refer to an antiquated civil law of stoning. This is actually understandable, for, in fact, there are only six general moral laws, namely, the last six of the Ten Commandments. I hope this brief refresher course helps you a bit. (I do understand, again however, that asking an atheist to do theology would be like asking Charles Darwin to do biology.)

On another note, you got upset with me didn't you? I can tell by the tone of your last letter. But it seems that this was not simply directed toward me, but the method of my argument. You assume that my reasoning is circular. Okay, but I say that yours is, too. I appeal to Scripture, and you appeal to reason. You have no brute facts for you position, and I have no brute facts for mine. So we both are arguing in a circle, so what! The question is whose circle is logical and whose is illogical?

Concerning the age of the earth, the atheists are quick to point to science. Now, even in the discussions among Christians, there is much to be said about this. There exists such a thing as theistic evolution that allows for such hypothesis of a primordial earth that has existed for billions of years. Listen, I fear that while I choose to debate at length those who hold such a position, I do think an important fact is missed when studying the Scriptures.

Let me explain it like this, Charles: Which came first, the chicken or the egg? Now I know what you Naturalists would say. They would begin to break forth into sporadic episodes of biological glossolalia stating that the entrance of protoplasm and matter merged with spontaneous combustible energy that attached to RNA before self-replicating by unique order, which proceeded to create a series of flagellum which, in turn, was able to reproduce while being structured by the various heatings of the imminent global system, which was a cause for random selection, which gave birth to a single-cell amphibias organism by which the creature began to internally reproduce by means of an interior egg that through time became an outer egg, as the sea level began to subside and as oxygen expanded. As you stated earlier, chance plus 4.5 billions years can do a lot, even scrambling an egg.

But we Christians who believe in a 7-Day Theory say that God created an Old Earth. What do I mean? I mean that when the earth was created, it had the features of old age built-in. Similarly, when the chicken was created (before the egg), it was a fully grown chicken. Likewise, the first man was created as a fully grown human being. This special quality of age gives credence to the uniqueness of creation, which points to the eternal Creator. Indeed, everything he made reflects himself in some capacity.

I hope I didn't go too far in my presuppositions for you. But don't we all have them?

You are loved by me.

J.J.

Dear Charles,

Well, hello Friend. I'm excited to hear of your coming to town next month. I'm glad that you will be staying for an entire month. I'll make a deal with you. We'll devote one night of the week to discuss theism and atheism. I love our conversations, but I love you more and do not want our discussions to get in the way of enjoying our time together.

You didn't have any questions in your last letter, but you did say that you feel that any belief in a personal God is similar to believing in a celestial dictator. You and many other atheists hate the idea of having a God watching over you and telling you what to do. I tell you, we men sure do like the idea of absolute autonomy.

Well, I must infer that when you are a member of the sheriff's family, you view him quite differently than the other townspeople do. We Christian see the sheriff as our Father, while the fugitives do not want to see him at all.

But listen to this, you say you don't like the idea of a divine dictator, but do you like the idea of a human one better? Are Idi Amin, Kim Jong-il, Joseph Stalin, Adolf Hitler, and Saddam Hussein better choices than a God who clothes the grass, feeds the birds, and provides sustenance for all living creatures? You tell me.

My friend, someone will always rule over you. When one rejects God he, in fact, places himself in God's position. I try not to use the classical apologetics of Aquinas too often when discussing these things, but I will use Anselm of Canterbury. Truly, if God is not the greatest thing one can conceive, then man himself is! If man is, he is worthy of worship. And you will find the most depraved men willing to fill that position.

And in closing, my friend, I dare say that atheism is only a product of free thought. But when no one is free, will the atheist still cling to his beliefs? (Or will he cry out, "*Eli, Eli, lama sabachthani*"?)

We'll talk more. I'll be picking you up at 3:30 at the station.

J.J.

Dear J.J.,

The women of XYZ University are very kind. Just look at my picture as a reminder of how kind they are. I sometimes feel as though I am taking advantage of their kindness. Then the check comes, and I'm reminded that they may have ulterior motives.

I was left confused by my lack of understanding of the Ten Commandments, but that's expected for an atheist who speaks directly and stands in the open. It's confusing to be an atheist, because one Christian group fights to put the Ten Commandments in a court, but group tells me that I'm wrong about what the Ten Commandments are. It's difficult to defend the Ten Commandments, when after 2000 years Christians worldwide still don't have a consensus on what the Bible teaches about them.

You suggested that atheists have no "brute" facts for their position, while admitting that you too have no "brute" for yours. This position you have taken can actually lead to much progress in our discussions. The whole of science is at odds with religion. It's not that a god can't exist, and that's not the atheist's position either. It's that the information at hand does not lend credence to any god. Only one man in history has fully understood the Bible and Evolution as a theory. That was Darwin. He waited 20 years to publish *On the Origin of Species*, because he knew what it would mean to Christians. We know that the biblical description of the natural world is not correct. Just consider cloud formations and tornados as examples (cf. Nahum 1:3: "His way is in the whirlwind and the storm, and clouds are the dust of his feet"). So the next time you have a headache and reach for acetaminophen, remember that it was put together by the chemistry and biology that you repudiate. My "brute" evidence is that you'll put that pill in your mouth rather than praying for the pain to stop. Additionally, there's a 97% chance that the scientist that designed the pill was an atheist.

When I was a child, I didn't know the world. I needed my

parents to guide me to safety. As an adult, they have let me go to live my life and make my own mistakes. No one needs to rule over me anymore. There have always been despots in the world. The government model that seems to work the best is one wherein the people rule the government, and not the other way around. In my travels to Europe in the Czech Republic, Netherlands, Denmark, etc., I've found it refreshing that their governments weren't there to control the people. I find it so fascinating that you speak of "someone" always ruling over me when the countries with no singular rulers have the least crime and the happiest populations.

You asked when would an atheist cry out for God. Something that I haven't told you is that the current job I am working at--to pay for college—is quite dangerous, namely, erecting tower cranes. In the times that I've faced the possibility of death, I've focused on how to prevent it rather than submitted to it. Remember when I went down on your dad's Motorcycle at 55 mph at age 16? I didn't pray then either. I tucked in as tight as I could, and the tree that my helmet glanced off (cracking the helmet) just barely cleared. I wonder what the result would have been if I started to pray instead? I can't apologize to your Father enough. That will always embarrass me. It's a shame that I put upon myself, and no one can forgive me for it. That's a hard part about being an atheist. At least Jesus will lift your guilt.

I must run now. Class starts soon! What's your favorite beverage these days? I must bring some for our visit. Will we be able to see old friends when I'm home as well? I wonder if the ladies back home will take pity on my hunchback.

Regards,
Charles

Dearest Charles,

Well hello once again. I daresay we've been writing so much that I hope you are not falling behind in your studies. As a matter of fact, I wouldn't mind it too much if you did choose to leave XYZ University. That school is known around the hometown as Wormwood University. Fancy that you chose it, but I trust the work of the Sovereign is even in this. (Even the great C.S. Lewis was also in your position.)

Ahh, the checks keep coming! Hilarious! I see you have kept that sense of humor as always. You rarely surprise me. (Not counting...) Well please know that I've taken an interest in a young damsel as well. She is astute, both aesthetically and intellectually. You know I always had a way with the ladies. Was it my dashing demeanor, my honed sense of humor, or my luring good looks? Nay. It has always been my humility.

Well, back to the issues you addressed in your last letter. It seems to you that there is no evident cohesion in biblical doctrine. I do understand the confusion. But the existence of different views concerning such non-essential issues doesn't negate truth.

Personally, I believe that the perspicuity of divine truth always is multi-faceted while uniquely interpreted. But you know all too well the indisputable doctrines of the Christian faith, Sola Scriptura, Sola Fides, Solus Christus, Sola Gratia, Soli Deo Gloria. These are our bedrocks.

Back to the multifaceted nature of God's truth. It's kind of like that issue of unity in diversity that you atheists shut your mouths at. We Christians say that the world is diverse but unified, because this reflects the glory of its Creator, the Trinity. The Atheists have no answer for this, and neither did Darwin. Irreducible Complexity does well to undermine the whole theory of natural selection. But I guess even naturalists can be unified in their diverse rejections of truth. Even Darwin said, "Ignorance more commonly begets confidence than does knowledge." (I can't believe that I just quoted Darwin positively. Amazing!)

Well, concerning the other topics of your last epistle. You are much more attuned to the things of Darwin than I am, but doesn't Dr. Michael Behe takes Darwin to task at his own wager by the argument of irreducible complexity? And could it be true that naturalistic biologists MUST presuppose atheism before they commence their work. (If they did not presuppose atheism they could not do science, right?) It's kind of like that aspirin you mentioned. If I presuppose that I must find a cure for my headache without aspirin, I'm sure I'll find one (even if it means cutting my head off).

And listen, Charles, I am thankful for Charles Gerhardt for inventing the aspirin. But I am more thankful for the one who originally provided the coal tar for him to do so. (Town rumor has it that you were named after Gerhardt. I guess your dear mom and pop had an inkling to the pain relief they might need to raise such a boy as you. Ha!)

I must admit, I chuckle a bit at your reference to Denmark, Netherlands, and the Czech Republic, and their peaceful dispositions. You know I am a novice when it comes to travel, but more refined when it comes to history. Have you not read the history of these nations? They all were established by wars and bloodshed. And history proves that at some point, they will once again possess the necessity of such a defense. Yes, Charles, replace the "Divine Dictator" and you will see a Depraved One. (I believe that being in the West too long has spoiled both of us.)

And must you bring up my dad's motorcycle? I have tried so hard to forget about that! I tell you, if one thing almost tore our friendship asunder (besides the tree branch that you barely missed) was that incident. I prayed desperately that day that you would not be seriously hurt. I also prayed that my father would not disembowel you. It's empirical proof, I do say, that both prayers were answered. As far as the guilt is concerned, I look forward to reading a work on the evolution of emotions. Anything you can suggest?

And in closing, my palate for a good drink remains the same. I enjoy a Chardonnay on occasion or a cold ale after I'm paid from my custodial job. Gone are the days of social drinking since you have left, my friend.

Truly Yours,

J.J.

Dear J.J.

The cold ales? Now, who would not like those? Refreshing to the palate and invigorating for the humor. I'll be sure to bring some along. Last night I enjoyed a couple of brews with dinner. Would you believe that the restaurant had 160 options on tap?

I so wish that you could have joined me on my travels through Europe. This summer I will take in the experience once again. While the traditional father of Czech nation was King Charles, a noted Christian, and the Danish history of pillaging was during a time of Christian leadership, it is all but gone. Some might even suggest the new found lack of religion is why they are peaceful now. The burning of Jan Hus at the stake, running monarchies, buying one's way into heaven and the ilk certainly left a poor taste in their mouths. The final straw was Hitler's actions and a church that supported them. I'm so glad that they apologized though. I wonder how many Hail Mary's the Pope had to say. Well, all of that was so long ago, I'm sure that they have been behaving well since then. I don't know, I've been studying so much that I feel like I'm living under a rock sometimes.

I spoke of taking acetaminophen in my last letter. Then you referred to my namesake. He was a clever old chemist. My young mother would be so proud of me thinking for myself. Sadly, the older mother she is now isn't quite the same. There are two men credited with the modern acetaminophen pill. Julius Axelrod is one of those men and a noted atheist. I feel so proud of the great number of accomplishments of such a minority group. The Nobel Prize list is a veritable Who's Who of Atheists! I wonder why God doesn't bless more Christians with these talents, or even on a statistically even playing field. The mysteries of our Lord are difficult to comprehend.

Have you read this great book by Lee Strobel called *The Case for a Creator*? Fantastic book! And I do mean fantastic! One of my neighbors who is a pastor gave it to me. It was such a generous thing to do, and the value of it plays out at least weekly. Dr. Behe, and all of the Discovery Institute Leadership, is interviewed in it. It was refreshing to hear their arguments firsthand. Otherwise, I would only be able to hear things like the judge in the Kitzmiller vs. Dover case citing Behe as the reason Intelligent Design is not based on Science. When I heard his argument for the irreducible complexity of the eye, I thought "Wow! Great Argument!" After some thought, the animals on the ocean floor came to mind. It's dark down there, and they only have photo receptors. Then, as we move up closer to the light, the eyes become more and more complex. I certainly hope that this doesn't create a problem for Dr. Behe's credibility. He's such a nice man and trying to do so much good with science.

Emotions are a stumper, too. I wonder if creating a bond in a family or herd would drive the herd to work together and protect one another. The more a family is willing to do to protect one another, the longer they might live to reproduce and pass on those genes? Hence, emotions hold family together and shape behaviors that eventually become societal laws. In the US, we are faced with one, as one of the only countries selfish enough to worry about money over life. I certainly hope that the '*Conservative Right*' would understand that Jesus told the rich young ruler to give away his money and follow him. But at least in death, they will get to enjoy his glory. I wonder how thinking of the greater good breaks down by different religions and how it affects the different countries' treatment of their people? I'll have to look into that one day.

The motorcycle... (sigh). I'm glad that you prayed that your father wouldn't disembowel me. Your prayer saved my life! Without your prayer, who knows how he might have snapped. I mean, it was a brand new motorcycle! You are a lifesaver! I'm sure Jesus would have let me get the deserved punishment if it wasn't for your influence.

I'm off to the store for that cold ale. It is New Year's Eve, and

I'll need to practice in order to keep up with you in the consumption. Maybe with your time off and me being in college, we'll be able to enjoy the evening without you having to carry me home!

Regards,

Charles

Dear Charles,

Happy New Year, 2010 Years after the coming of the Blessed One, give or take 4-6 years! (It's amazing to think that our entire system of dating is based upon the birth of a man from Galilee.)

What's going on friend? I hope you and your girl Mary are doing well together. I'm guessing you told her about me. And I'm shocked to hear that she is only an agnostic and not a full blown atheist. Well, maybe she we'll rub off on you, and you will begin to come back to the light.

The damsel I told you about informed me that she just wants to be friends now. I must accept that. She is truly a jewel though. And sometimes jewels are meant to be enjoyed from a distance. I'm a realist though. If she never rest in my arms, it's okay, as long as she rests in His.

I believe it is time we address the subject of epistemology. That's a big word by the way. But the only way we can know anything is by reason or revelation. Either a man can figure something out by himself or he must have it revealed to him. We Christians are obviously on the side of revelation. Is there anything I know that wasn't revealed to me?

I must speak briefly for a moment on science and reason. We Christians are so misconstrued when it comes to the relationship between the two. Never would I as a devout theist suggest that reason and science have no place in the realm of reality. God forbid. The very science of science is a testimony to reason and the power of the human mind. But yet, we, as devout believers in the Bible, believe that there can or will be no discovery by science that will go contrary to revelation as found in Holy Writ. (And if science appears to be contrariwise, further study will prove otherwise.) The only thing absolute about science is its absolute limitation. Thank God for science, but let the believer also thank God that science is not the *sine qua non*! (I learned that phrase in seminary!)

Your professor might say, "Reason is the ultimate criteria for understanding reality." But even if that is true, they just told it to you, therefore it was revealed. (Ha!) It was probably their professor that told that to them. If you say science is the criteria, then science is your revelation. You see where I'm going. And really, if reason was the standard, then the means by which one reasons must be discussed. If I use my senses to help me reason, then there, too, must exist some standard of testing my reason. Even greater than that, if I reason that anything is true, by what criteria should one examine my reasoning?

No, Charles. What I described above does not seem fit cohesively in an epistemological system. We say everything is revealed. God revealed himself through creation, and creation reveals the one who made it. Therefore, your reason is really the revealed work of God. Your very ability to reason gives you a reason to believe in reason which is itself revealed.

Man, you've got me talking like this. (I never was good at apologetics.) Listen, I just don't see how your worldview can be consistent epistemologically, ontologically, or ethically. (Obviously not morally.) Just listen to what I'm saying, and you'll see the reason and revelation in it.

Your Friend,
J.J.
P.S. My Professor here at the seminary said that atheism is not an intellectual choice, but a morally volitional choice. How do you respond?

Dear J.J.,

Your letter finds me up early on this New Year Day! It is a great joy that we get to enjoy another New Year. I hope that the evening kept you safe and with a smile. Mary was not impressed with my snoring on the couch. It seems that the evening isn't neatly as fun as it used to be. Perhaps if we lived in a warmer and drier climate, these evenings would have a greater draw.

The ladies have escaped your grasp? (They always seem to, don't they?) You'll have to search for new treasures. The excitement of new love is so consuming that the pain is numbed. Maybe you can find a Love Potion; preferably #9, to assist you in your quest. I kid, I kid. I hope the pain finds a new home soon.

You speak of the science of the Bible and the eventual proof that will come that God was correct. I recall being confused as to a story of Nebuchadnezzar's dream of a tree that was so tall that it could be seen from anywhere on the Earth. I pictured myself standing on the opposite side of the globe and pondered how tall that tree would have to be for me to see it? It of course was both a dream and a representation of how the king saw himself. But then it happened again in Matthew 4:8: "Again, the devil took him to a very high mountain, and showed him all the kingdoms of the world and the glory of them. There are many biblical references to a flat Earth, but I have seen many pictures and videos that contradict the Bible. Of course, the notion of a flat Earth was generally known to not be the true amongst the learned by the time of the writing of the Bible. I hope that having become a skeptic doesn't prevent me from seeing the light. But I can't help but think that the learned were not the authors of the Bible.

Your seminary professor does speak of some truths in life. Many of today's youth are choosing atheism, because they don't find the what happened last 9 years reasonable. The choice to wage an unprovoked war by a man who claimed God told him to do so is not acceptable to many of them. Stem cell arguments, abortion arguments, anti-science attitudes (e.g, those concerning global warming that clearly supporting large corporations who profit by ignoring science and the public interest), etc., do drive people away. So, in this instance, I would agree with your professor and those who reject those who would subject others to the rules of their religion. Teddy Roosevelt, a devout man of God, handled it correctly when asked to put "In God We Trust" on the money. "My own feeling in the matter is due to my very firm conviction that to put such a motto on coins, or to use it in any kindred manner, not only does no good, but does actual harm, and is, in effect, irreverence and even comes dangerously close to sacrilege. It seems to me eminently unwise to cheapen such a motto by putting it on coins, just as it would be to cheapen it by using it on postage stamps or in advertisements." If Mr. Bush could have recognized his role and duties, he would not have created the White House Office of Faith-Based and Neighborhood Partnerships and overstepped many other boundaries. The representation as a Christian while ignoring the rule of law has been a great problem for drawing the youth to God.

A story that you might not recall was my learning to accept the death of my great-grandfather. It's such a long story, but I'll be brief. I was young, 5 or 6. My grandfather died, and it was the first death of someone close to me. Then my favorite aunt died shortly thereafter. It was difficult to accept. I had to learn that life ends, and matchbox cars are eternal so get back to it! The next Easter in Sunday School, I questioned the resurrection by stating, "People don't come back to life." For interrupting, I found myself with my nose in the corner. While I wanted to fit in and get along in life, this was the turning point. I hope that this doesn't sully your memories of our upbringing in religion. Sometimes families won't accept the difference and neither will friends. I just wanted to be normal.

I have a question. Does your professor mean that people choose atheism in order to not have to be moral? If so, I would direct you back to prison population rates per capita in Japan, Denmark, etc., versus Iran, US, Saudi Arabia, etc. Look at the abortion rates of the US of 21 per 1000 in the US versus 5 per 1000 in the Netherlands. Divorce rates are the lowest at 21% as compared to 34% by the non-denominational. This leads to more two-parent households and stronger family units as well. I wonder what measure one would use to evaluate the immorality of an atheist.

The mountains are calling my name. Nothing straightens out my hunchback like a long 10-mile hike up a mountain. My dog was bred to hunt lions, and he needs the exercise. I wish that you could see him in the hunt of a deer. Like the wind he is. My 4-mile runs are too slow and too short for him. I'll have to bring him back with me so you can take him on a marathon for me. Enjoy the day and Happy New Year to you!

Regards,
Charles

My Beloved Charles,

Maranatha!

A new year with new opportunities has apprehended us. Let us be thankful for another day, another breath, another chance to converse by pen.

So how was your hike? You know ever since you have left for XYZ University, I seem to lack the motivation and vigor I once had to exercise. Oh, don't get my wrong. I am still a fine specimen of man, but I do say that I have taken on a more circular and spherical shape. I'm round now. Let's just say this, if I dressed up for a costume party as a basketball, I wouldn't need to purchase much material. (Ha! Self-deprecating humor is the mark of true humility.) But all is well. Hopefully, when you return for your visit we can once again hike as we did as youngsters. (By the way, have you stopped smoking yet?)

I do admit, your last letter disappointed me. You truly failed to address the subject of epistemology or the discord of the atheistic worldview concerning knowledge. Is it reason, revelation, or both? I feel that whatever system you pick, your worldview will not allow you to follow it consistently to its core.

The moral argument is the constant beating of the drum for atheists. You say, "Look at the Crusades, look at the Inquisition, look at George W. Bush (that's a new one), and look at divorce rates among Christians." I confess that while I understand your argument (for it is really the 1 of the 2 pillars of the atheist movement), the beating of the drum is becoming weaker. Let us remember that only 2% of the world's population consider themselves devout atheists, and maybe 10% of that fall into the category of agnostics. Our earliest encounters with the so-called "atheists" did not occur until the 18th century. (I know you may remind me of the Epicureans, but I say they should be classified more as deists rather than as atheists.)

So, in the age of the Earth (I know you mentioned James

Ussher's 6000-year theory), there is no clear Christian consensus concerning this, though my own personal study into biblical genealogies gives me a 14,000-year time frame, with the flood occurring around 5000 B.C. But during this 14,000 year history, we see almost no pure form of atheism until the last 300 years. Free thought breeds skepticism, and skepticism begets the sisters of agnostism and atheism. So, when you make moral charges against the religion of the Christians, or any religion per se , the atheist ALWAYS points to religion as the motivation and not to the depravity of man, his lust, greed, or desire for political power as motivation. That is unbalanced, wouldn't you say?

As far as the resurrection of life is concerned, your childhood experience is unfortunate, and it troubles me. A child with questions should be listened to and not ostracized. But as far as the resurrection of life, do not we see that every spring? Ahh...the glories of the new life proceeding forth from deadness! How about a seed being buried in the ground, but only to rise again later as something new and glorious? Or what about that recent story in the Herald Sun News of the mother and her newborn that died during birth and came back to life this past Christmas.

But most importantly, what about the Man from Galilee who died and rose again? What about the Old Testament prophecies that predicted this? What about the 11 disciples who were willing to be killed and tortured rather than denying that they had seen Him? What about C.S. Lewis, who, formerly devoted to your system, was surprised by joy after embracing the truth of this resurrection? Yes, dear Charles, Someone has been raised back to life.

And in closing, you mention the deaths of your grandfather and aunt—hard losses for anyone, especially for a dear soul such as yourself. (But I remember that neither of them were atheists.) I am reminded of the absolute terror that invades the atheists at the moment of their deaths. A biographer of Thomas Hobbs describes Hobbs' death in these words: "When the atheist Hobbs drew near to death, he declared loudly, 'I am about the take a leap into the dark.'" Voltaire was overpowered with grief. He called in all of his unbelieving friends, and his biographer records, "He cursed them to their faces, and he loudly repeated, 'Begone, begone, it is you that have brought me to my present condition. Leave me, I say, begone. What a wretched glory is this which you have produced for me.'" For two months, he was tortured with such great agony that it caused him at times to gnash his teeth in impotent rage against God and man. At other times, in plaintive accents, he pleaded, "Oh, Christ, oh, Christ, oh, Lord Jesus," and then, at last, he turned his face and cried, "I die abandoned by God and man."

Oh Charles, love contraineth...but it also waiteth. I wait for your return to who you were.

In Sincerest Love,
J.J.

Dear J.J.,

Great to see that you had some time to relax and write today. The hike today provided me with the chance to test out a new insulated rain coat for myself, and another for the dog. It was a nice 9-miler with waterfalls, a lake, and a tree growing through the grille of an Old Model A truck used years ago during the original logging effort. It's an interesting view into the past as the tree is likely a second generation growth since the originals were fallen. I only wish that it wasn't raining so hard so that I would have had the DSLR with me to properly capture the find. Alas, when the sun returns, I'll capture it for posterity.

It's a pity that you are missing out on exercise. Age gathers quickly, and youth is buried by extra weight. I should know. I can't forget the days when I carried an extra 50 lbs. But do you remember in elementary when you were a little on the chunky side? In our school's Thanksgiving play, the teacher asked you if you if you could play the role of the turkey. That was terrible. (Terribly funny, I do say.)

As for my nicotine addiction, the cravings are still triggered by the combination of water, barley and hops. I may be down to a pack a year, so hopefully, it isn't causing too much damage. It's been a month and a half since my last cigarette.

The question concerning the source and rise of atheism is one with a different answer for each person. I can only answer it for myself. I've noted that my journey began when I was presented with information that I knew not to be true. I suppose the information was revelation on both points, and the conclusion was my reasoning. I didn't know what it meant at 6 years old, but time and my consistent rejection of claims such as the flood had led me to this. No one told me that the flood wasn't true, it simply didn't make sense. Growing up, I didn't know any atheists, and I would be hard pressed to find one that was a teacher to this day. But I was clearly a non-believer by the time I was in high school. College has given me the tools to know why I reject the tenets of religion. In these cases, I suppose it's revelation of the information with me reasoning toward the conclusion.

The singular event that provoked me to become active with my studies was what happened on September 11th, 2001. The rhetoric of "One Nation Under God" drove me out of my hole. More specifically, William Donohue, a Rabbi, and a Islamic cleric (I know, it sounds like I'm setting up a joke!) were on a talk show, Larry King, as I recall off hand, and speaking of the three religions being born from the Old Testament. This was a shock to me as I hadn't searched beyond the Old and New Testament. I didn't know about Judaism or Islam. The three coming from one book lead me to the question, "Then aren't they talking about one God?" So revelation led me to a question.

There is a consistency here. I have pieces of information that led me to questions about the knowledge being presented. I can choose what I see in life, the natural world, and what I have experienced, or I can choose faith, i.e., to believe that what I can't see, taste and experience, is true. My personality is that of needing a tangible answer, and so I reject the ethereal. The same goes for UFO's, Bigfoot, and even the reliable American car!

Atheists are new to the world for a number of reasons. Two hundred years ago, calling a man an atheist was an insult. Teddy Roosevelt referred to Thomas Paine as a "filthy little atheist". When men saw the world as a naturalist, they couldn't conceive of how the world was created. So, they claimed to be deists. Deists seek reason and natural explanations, but proposed that a God created the world then moved and had nothing else to do with the world or us. Some call this a watchmaker god. Jefferson, Madison, Washington, Paine, Ethan Allen and others believed this. Given modern science, I would argue that all of these men would have been atheists. Of course, without a time machine we would both be left quote-mining and wasting time.

You wrote, "What can I know that wasn't revealed to me?" You can discover it. Prior to Darwin, no one had put forth the idea of evolution. Robert Goddard used trial and error to understand how to shoot a rocket straight and reliably. If revelation was the only way to know anything, then the first men would have known everything that could be known. Since there were less people, so those people would have necessarily been geniuses. When you consider the ability to share information, which means that men within a given society must have known all of this information. It doesn't ring true unless I've missed the point. But it wouldn't be the first time!

So, you contend that the earth is 14,000 years old. How do you account for coral reefs having rings just like trees and the fact that Vermont has a reef that dates back 450 million years? I could go on and on, but ring dating on reefs is like that of trees. It's so accurate that when possible, scientists would use ring dating to cross reference radio carbon dating. I really enjoyed it when a priest in Bill Maher's movie *Religulous* said, "Modern science began in 1500 years after the writing of the Bible. There is no science in the Bible. The Catholic Church has a division that takes advice from a scientific panel that helps them understand what is going on and how it impacts them. From there, they adjust and decide what parts of the Bible should be seen as poetry, parable, and literal. I would suggest that this is the "God of the gaps" and that eventually the entire text will be recognized as poetry only. I find it interesting that Peter's own church has been so backed into a corner that they are giving up ground.

I must find some sleep. The storms are blowing in, and I may not get sound sleep tonight. I do enjoy a good storm. In this part of the country, acceptance of the weather is compulsory. I hope that I addressed your question of revelation or reason.

Regards,
Charles

My good friend Charles,

I must start off by first thanking you for your last letter. I'll get around to addressing my reply concerning reason in a later letter. (This epistemology subject must be sifted until either reason or revelation is crowned ultimate. But that's for another day.)

Are you keeping up with pop culture nowadays? Please say yes for my sake. Many of the seminarians are such studious students that they know nothing of politics, sports, or *Jon & Kate Plus 8*. I believe that these things make for good conversations to say the least.

So what is the music taste at XYZ University? You know that music truly reflects the underlying thought of the culture. Study the music of the late 60s and early 70s, and you'll find the freedom of rebellion, freedom of uprising, and a desire for change. Gil Scott Heron speaks well of that culture.

I can thankfully say that the African-American tide of musical art has turned in from the former direction. Gone are the days the 1990's reign of the malevolent, misogynistic, and murderous melodies of MC Eiht, NWA, and Lynch Hung. No, we have replaced those with a more refined brand of corporate entrepreneurship and sensuality that defines the mainstream such as Rihanna and Young Jeezy. (Jeezy? I thought my name was strange.) Is this type of music better than the former? I would say no; it's just the desire for absolute autonomy expressed in a different form.

With the tide of thought that pervades XYZ University, I would guess that your school's top musical choices are System of a Down, (are they still on hiatus?) Coldplay, Greenday, and a bit of classical. These acts seem to be inclusive enough to welcome all thought. (Speaking of classical, it's amazing how the atheists have such a taste for the finer forms of music, but not so much for the universal chord that holds all notes together.) I once read somewhere that there are only 7 core basic notes in music. You know 7 is the biblical number denoting perfection… you see where I'm going.

I remember that you always leaned toward a more soft rock or a folksy side of music. Do you remember when I bought you your first Peter Frampton album, and you almost kissed me in the mouth? (I still believe that my first girlfriend left me because of that.) Or that Simon and Garfunkel album that I surprised you with one Christmas? Those two gifts will forever link us at the hip.

Wait until you see what I bought for your return. I'll give you a hint; it will not be another Peter Frampton album. (My love life is hard enough the way it is.)

Until next time, my dear friend.

(I find myself quite often looking forward to your letters. Thank you.)

J.J.

P.S. Tell me, how is Mary doing; are you treating her well? Remember not to feed her after midnight and keep her away from water. Isn't she from Mogwai? (Ha!)

Dear Charles,

I appreciate the short letter you wrote and your question, "Could anything be proven in science that would cause me to abandon my faith in God?" That's a fair question, and I dare not place myself in some circle and immediately say no.

I'll say, yes, there is something in science that could make me switch sides. Now when we talk about science, I'm assuming we're discussing the Darwinian natural selection method. Well, if science could show me a baby that could change its own diaper, then I would renounce my Christian faith. Does that sound comical? I'm serious. Show me a newborn baby that can change its own diaper, change its own bottle, or fix its own food, then I'd be riding with you, Bro!

What I'm saying is this: if evolution and natural selection are true, then there had to be a first baby. Now I know what you're going to say; you're going to tell me something about a missing link, or that spontaneous generation didn't occur, or that it was probably an amphibian creature or something. (I know the basic premises of your *faith* in atheism.) Ok. Well, who fed the first monkey-fish/cat-man baby? You know that no fish-monkey/cat-man baby can feed itself! Who's going to get that monkey/cat-man-fish baby catnip or get him/it banana formula? Come on! I'm being serious here; this is not meant to be funny.

To be honest, I don't know if that would be natural selection, because there is nothing natural about a flagellum-monkey/fish-man baby. I get scared just thinking about that. And even if it was natural, who would select that? So until science can show me a missing link or tell me how the first missing link fed itself, then I'll keep my keys to the kingdom.

Your Friend

J.J.

Dear Charles,

Hey friend! So you're saying that the question you asked in the last letter was addressed in one of your classes by a classmate. Ok, I got you. I understand. It was a valid question, and I'll accept it.

The question was, "Why would God need to threaten people with judgment and hell." Well, there are a couple ways that could be addressed. The term "threaten" is somewhat foreign to the biblical concept. So I'll use "warn." (Threaten has the connotation of fearing an action instead of a person. Both Old and New Testaments advocate love as God's motive for his giving (cf. John 3:16). God would rather have you love him than fear his punishment. But when one does love him, one would no longer fear punishment.)

Well, it is true that the God of the Bible does warn people about hell. And to be honest with you, I'm mighty thankful that he does! I would hate to die and have God tell me, "I forgot to warn you about this place you're about to go to, but it's hot." No, please tell me in advance. It's like going to that Geno's Steaks, and the clerk tells you that there's a 3-hour wait. I'm glad she tells me that, so now I can go to Pat's Steaks. It informs me, so I can make another and usually more convenient decision. Atheism, on the other hand, warns me of nothing. Because it is theory, it can't warn me of anything.

I'm glad God warns of hell so many times in the Bible. It's a warning me to make a more convenient decision. (You know we're both from Georgia, but we never did handle heat too well.)

As for me, you should know that I am struggling in my Greek class. I thought I was pretty good at languages until now. I guess Pig Latin doesn't count in a seminary.

LrightA, llI alkT aterL.

Your Friend,

J.J.

Dear Charles,

First and foremost, I want to say that I'm sorry about you and Mary breaking up. I know I joked with you a lot, but really, I'm sad to hear about that. But from your last letter, you seem to be doing alright with it. I see you continued on with your line of questioning. And I knew that somewhere soon, you would bring up the issue of pain.

So, you asked if God is all powerful, why he would allow pain. Well, for one, I don't really have to tell you the expected answer. I mean, you know what the Christian faith says about evil and how its origins are found in the sin of mankind. You know that. But I want to address it from a different perspective.

Charles, what is the point of pain in the nervous system? Pain is meant to be an indicator of an internal problem. You remember that time we were skateboarding at your mom's house and you tried to imitate Tony Hawk's 720 degree rotation invert? But you tried it in the backyard pool, and your foot got stuck in the drain, and it was less of a 720 and more of a 911. A 911 emergency, that is. Well, it was that pain that indicated that your fibula was fractured, and, therefore, you needed special attention. It seems to me that the world's pain is meant to be a wake up call to a greater and more serious internal problem.

I know most people don't look at it like that. It easy to give theological sermons and stuff like that, but in reality, that doesn't help anybody that is really hurting. But to know that all of our pain is meant to direct us to God, who is our 911, makes the hurt a little more bearable, for we know that help is on the way.

I'm praying for you,

J.J.

Dearest Charles,

If I may, I will save the warm and cordial greetings for a later time. I must immediately with the issue at hand.

In your last letter, you gave me more than a share of the atrocities that have been done either by religion or the followers of religion. I mean you started from Cain and Abel and went all the way to September 11th. You say, "Why is a religion a good thing, when religion has this to show for it?"

First, Charles, I do not speak for every religion. You know what my faith is, so I cannot speak for what Muslims, Mormons, Buddhists, or any other sects. But I do admit that much evil has been done by the followers of my faith as well. This cannot be denied.

Well, let me start off like this. In your last letter, I see you wrote with a pencil and not your usual pen. You wrote with a lead pencil. Do you know what else lead is used to make? It is used to make most bullets. Lead which can be used for wires, pipes, or pencils, and it can also be used to create bullets. Now, a bullet can be used for good or evil. It can be used for good, when the police uses it to stop a criminal from hurting a child. It can be used for evil, when that criminal aims a gun at the child. So, we would say from the onset that lead is good, but it is how it is used that makes it evil.

I daresay that my faith is good. Oh yes, it is of the highest good, because of its divine origin. But I also say that men are so bad that we take that which is good and use it for evil. It doesn't make the religion bad, because bad men use it, and it does not make it good, because good men use it. (Who is really good anyway?) But what it does show, when bad men use Christianity, is that Christianity is true. "How does it prove Christianity is true?" you ask. The heart of man is so deceitfully wicked (as

Christianity states) that it will even use God's gift for such a purpose as evil. (But, man has been doing this all along.)

J.J.

P.S. If I don't write for a while, it's because I'm preparing for my finals.

Dear J.J.,

I hope you are well, my dear friend. Please forgive me for not writing for a while. I have found myself in a season of a financial strait. Don't worry though, for you know how undergrads always struggle in this area until financial aid comes in. I remember that you were so broke during your sophomore in year in college that you sold your plasma twice a day for week? Ha! I've never seen a paler black man in my life (excluding the King of Pop of course)! You would have done well to try out as an extra for one of those Twilight movies.

Listen, in lieu of the price of postage in sending numerous letters back of forth, I have a challenge for you and me. Write me a short thesis (from a purely philosophical standpoint) on the essence and nature of life. Address the big three issues: epistemology, ontology, and ethics. Please don't go overboard on the metaphysics. Remember I have read Aristotle, too. Please show me how reason and rationale can lead to any worldview that would point to revealed religions as the chasm of ultimate reality. I do not believe that a real and rational worldview can. (But who said Christians were rational?)

After I read yours, I will send you my anti-thesis. I promise to keep it brief while shrewdly disposing of your points and outlines. But who knows? Maybe you will write such a magnum opus that I will immediately bow the knee to my former Christian faith upon reading it. (I doubt it, unless you find an editor.)

Regards,

Charles

Two weeks later...

Dear Charles,

Per your request, I have written a short thesis on the essence of life from a purely philosophical standpoint. Your challenge to me was to see if pure philosophy could reasonably lead me to an apparent and succinct Christian worldview. You also say that you will write an anti-thesis to show how philosophy and reason always lead away from any modus operandi that suggests divine origin.

Before you read, please remember that I always loathed Philosophy. During my first two years in college, I still thought that Plato was the silly putty we played with as children.

Always in love,

J.J.

Life

A wise man once said, "There are three types of people in this world: me, you, and others." The quote's simplicity should produce a smile on anyone who encounters it. One probably may question just how wise this wise man actually was! But, in fact, there are (by the lowest common denominators) three ways in which one could choose to define and fulfill his existence.

The first of these ways is what I will classify as hedonism. This is the type of which the chief pursuit is sensuality. "Life, liberty, and the pursuit of carnal pleasures" would be the final words of their declaration. The second way of existence is that of the philosophy. Such philosophers are not always of a particular brand as were the Stoics and Epicureans, but those who possess a self-assessed or acquired worldview based solely or primarily upon reason. And finally, we have those that have engrafted themselves in the seams of religion.

The common belief concerning the latter two groups mentioned is that philosophy and religion go hand-in-hand. But this (in my understanding) is not true. It is altogether more common that the one who fits in the category of philosopher would include religion as a subcategory of philosophy rather than the reverse. However, my stated definition of philosophy and religion should settle that issue. Philosophy is intelligent imagination based on man's reasoning, while religion is claimed to be from direct divine revelation.

Being woven in faith or being bound by pleasure, you should be able to easily classify yourself. If you are neither of the two, then you would obviously fit into the realm of the philosopher. The truth is that you, in all subjectivity, define the world in metaphorical terms, comparing the world using phrases such as "life is like..."

So, I hope that by now you are able to identify yourself for the thesis' sake. If not, ask yourself this question, "Would you rather be right or feel good?" If you answer the latter you are not religious. Now ask yourself, "Is divine wisdom in a book or in the heart?" If you answer the former you are not a philosopher. Now let us dive into the benefits and hindrances of all types.

Hedonism

The hedonist pursues and persists in pure carnal satisfaction. He eats it like the sweetest candy. Childhood experiences should indicate, however, as mother always told us; too many sweets will cause sickness. This is especially true when the amount of ingestion increases by mass and quantity with every dosage.

This is the major restraint of hedonism: it can never be truly fulfilled, but only transferred to the next object of lust. While the immediate sensation of pleasure binds one to its pursuit, it pervades every other area of one's existentialism, which, in turn, defines the self-same existence.

Common Philosophy and Religion

"If it works you are seen as wise." To what type would this quote apply? This is the mantra of the pragmatic philosopher. Think about the most successful in the secular realm. These philosophers have formed an opinion of life, embraced it, and are now considered conquerors in the world's eyes?

Let us dissect the philosopher further. He is the one who has written his own manifesto of life and has hidden it in the shelf of his heart. And what does his critique of existence contain? Ask him! Ask yourself! The question is posed to those who live by their own self-imposed system of ethics and responses to the world around them. In all simplicity, philosophy is how you view the world and apply it to the life you live. This is also commonly known as your *worldview*. At this time, there are more worldviews than one can count. This is because each has variables, such as age, race, geography, experience, and time of history, that make each philosophy unique.

Philosophy has been called the heathen's religion. Aside from the obvious derogatory connotation of such a comparison, much can be gleaned from the statement. Philosophy is good, when it produces a desire for knowledge and a passion for one's fellow man. Countless philosophies can be credited for improving mankind's way of life. (I need not go into examples, unless the entire book is be dedicated to this subject alone.) Therefore, philosophy in the positive sense, can add much to the area of productivity.

The greatest resource of philosophy is the human mind. How great is this organ inside our heads? The mere complexity of a single wrinkle in our brain is infinitely more complex than all the computers of the world combined. Whether reasoning, creativity, or articulation, all these come from the same mind which in turn shapes our philosophy.

And what are philosophy's flaws? The most evident flaw is, ironically, its greatest strength. Even with the greatness of the mind, it is severely limited to be subjective at best. This is why any philosophy that is begotten from the mind of man can only be a philosophical or metaphysical hypothesis.

The second problem with the philosopher is that he has a pompous tendency to exalt himself above measure. The common subconscious response of the prosperous philosopher is that his way of thinking is correct. Just look at the man who not only possesses monetary excess but also health. And if this philosophy is solidified by the external, then those who have failed to meet this same standard would be wrong in their philosophy.

It could be said for this subject that many of the greatest philosophers are the most open-minded. I would not disagree with this, (especially saying that it's my theory). So, if we are to consider this valid, it must also mean that the most detrimental philosophies are those hailed by the closed-minded. If a man's dogma prevents him from responding to an immediate need of self or others, his perceived wisdom, then, becomes his crutch.

Finally, we approach the religious one. In reference to the religious, my application of the label is only to the devout. It seems more often than not that the man, who professes religion, in reality, has his life dominated by his own philosophy. Therefore for the sake of this exercise, one cannot categorize himself as such, unless his cognition is ruled by his faith.

What are the primary benefits of being religious? I'll begin by saying this: those who are devout in faith (barring fanatical ideology that would be classified as being in the realm of philosophy) can claim to be the most enlightened humans upon the face of the planet. Add to this the presence of character, and the argument is made that religion reveals the complete story of mankind. For it would preliminarily be seen that true religion should be the highest the *a priori* of mortal man.

What are religion's limitations? The answer can be posed in another question: "Is there absolute truth?" Philosophy, of course, will respond by saying that the answer is unattainable. But it is religion, on the other hand, that lifts up its voice to proclaim a resounding yes to that same question. That resounding assurance assures a resounding dilemma. That is, with a plethora of religions, it must be a reality that not all religions are true.

Therefore, almost all who claim religion are deceived. (Ahh… you say, could not more than one religion be true? I respond by asking, "Can two plus two *not* equal four?" If there is a logical deduction of reason in the sphere of odd and even numerals, would we be fools to expect or at least hope for the same in the realm of religion?)

I presume that this truth would not make an overwhelming dent to the conscience, if all religions only limited their promises to this brief earthly span. But it would not constitute religion, if only this life was involved. First century theologian Paul of Tarsus wrote, "Religion is profitable unto all things, having the promise of the life that now is, and of that which is to come." This concern for the afterlife is primarily the hope or fear of all its followers. So, placing oneself in such a belief system can leave one in the consequence of being absolutely wrong about absolute truth concerning this life and the next.

Another danger of religion is the possibility of self-contempt. This occurs when one begins to despise others in their present world surroundings. We would be hard-pressed if we had never come into contact with such a one that was totally disgusted with the human race in some sub-conscience degree that begins to ooze out through his words as puss does from a cankerous sore. We all might echo this man's sentiments when we ourselves are witnesses to the atrocities of mankind. But to condemn all mankind, while removing oneself from this present world order, only reveals an utter contempt of self.

The final danger of religion is similar to that of philosophy, but is possibly extremely more dangerous. That thing is pride displayed in the form of spiritual elitism. One is tempted to exalt himself above those whom he considers unenlightened or spiritually inferior.

Man's Hierarchy of Needs

After identifying the three specific modes of existence, one must now ask the questions of necessity: "Are all needs inclusive, exclusive? Or are they compatible or incompatible?" The truth is that regardless of what category one fits into, each type possesses the same basic needs. And, in all actuality, this hierarchy correlates perfectly with mankind's type of deductive ontology.

The three needs of all mankind are food, intercourse, and worship. Each need is true to its rudimentary definition, but also serves as a type of the intrinsic. But all three include the basic desires of all those born into the world with normal mental functions.

The primary need of mankind is the satisfaction of physical hunger. Mankind cannot exist without the nourishment that comes from food. Therefore, food fundamentally is the greatest motivation in life. A man works in order to eat and eats in order to work. This is a revolving door that has meat at the apex. This process undoubtedly must continue throughout life.

As previously stated, each desire is a type of its main body. Therefore hunger has been a shadow of deep emotional desires as well as of the carnal ones. This is why the need for acceptance, also known as love, is also parallel with such. In true psychological rigor and passion, every man is seeking some form of love.

This desire for acceptance is most commonly fulfilled in marriage. A spouse whether (male or female) is a microcosm of the world. A man desires this relationship to meet his internal need of acceptance. It is inherent in our lives that the process begins inside the cradle of acceptance. Then, as we become more mature, we use our newfound and newborn independence to immediately began seeking acceptance from external elements such as food, pacifier, or from being held. In all actuality, it seems to be a desire to enter once again (so to speak) into the womb, that one place wherein we were perfectly nurtured.

Intercourse is the second implied need of all living things. This begins in the sexual realm. Man is a sexual being. At the advent of puberty, this desire becomes almost as instinctive as one's need for food. Such a need is manifest in women by her craving to bear and rear offspring, and in men, by his desire to reproduce the image of himself (*imago sapiens*).

(Also accompanied with physical/sexual intercourse is sensuality. It would seem in most, many, or all, that the pleasurable aspect of intercourse would be an even greater motive for men and women coming together in this union. The question I'm suggesting is: what kind of need does sensuality fall under?)

The desire for pleasure is a cause-and-effect evidence of intercourse that reveals itself in the need for food. Because man has his sexual desire, which is also related to sensuality, he seeks to satisfy it through intercourse. Once the carnal delight has been tasted, or temporarily satisfied, the desire later becomes more aroused. This is why sex and acceptance are so intertwined with cognition.

We should know that intercourse is not limited to sexual terms only. The definition of intercourse is to engage oneself an intimate relationship. The initial act of intercourse is always with self. From the moment of adolescence, when we began to make cognitive decisions while responding to the setting around us, we are engaging in mental intercourse, i.e., conversing, contemplating, and engaging with self. This relationship, commonly known as self-dialogue continues throughout our entire existence.

The further our minds develop, the sooner we can begin to seek the types of intercourse that are beyond ourselves. This type of intercourse process is based upon evaluation, conclusion, and response. In all actuality, this is how philosophy begins. Usually, but not primarily, in our childhood, we begin to evaluate the world around us. As stated earlier, this evaluation is shaped by one's age, experience, etc. We are, again, at some point inclined to respond to a need, either personal or domestic, and even those that are universal. In this, we conclude our hypothesis (philosophy) to the need. And then, finally, we engage ourselves in response.

Societal and universal intercourse is commonly revealed in the type of life work one seeks to pursue. Usually based upon perception and one's early upbringing, a resolute desire for position or philanthropy is indicated. If external factors do not hinder this need, the individual will insert himself in the perceived system of his choice or necessity.

Once these needs are met, it is of a primal instinct that man seeks worship as the fundamental core. By the conviction of one's own conscience and the evidence of the solar system, we, at the most carnal level, recognize and sense deity and, therefore, seek worship. This is absolutely a part of every man, regardless of dogma.

While the world is not filled with devout believers of the divine deity, worship can also be transferred to something visible. This is commonly known as idolatry. Its definition is: the pursuit of metaphysical meaning via external criteria. This occurrence is displayed in every facet of mankind.

Worship in the divine sense has three motives from the standpoint of appearance. These are the fear, hope, or a combination of both. There exists in mankind a sub-conscious fear of divine retribution. (This can be independent of special revelation.) This fear leads man to seek reconciliation for the guilt that is manifest in his conscience. Such guilt is an extraordinary evidence of divine existence. In this instance, a man will seek to create or engraft himself in a religion that usually, by some prescribed work, bestows the promise of reconciliation.

Hope is essential to religion and worship. What is that hope? The answer is dependent upon the faith. But it usually consists of promises and benefits of life after death. The most common trigger for seeking or believing in a post-bios hope is the current depravity of the present world. It's all together likely that when the individual is born into great tribulation (either physical or emotional), his desire for worship will be aroused by the hope that there must be a *neo-cosmos* that is free from the current world order.

Self-Righteousness and Sorrow

Self worship always begets self-righteousness either consciously or subconsciously. This is altogether more common in philosophers than in the religious adherents. When one adheres to the belief in absolute truth he likely disqualifies himself from being a philosopher in practice. For if the philosopher believed that a fact relating to himself was absolute truth, would not his life be devoted to that truth? And if his life was devoted to such a truth, would it not be an act of worship? His three basic desires would, then, be centered on that truth. He, in turn, would be quasi-religious. But we know this is not the case for the philosopher. Therefore, this group can not respond. This worship desire, when turned inwardly upon self, would thereby create self-righteousness.

So what really is self-righteousness? It is the belief and practice that one's self is the highest authority. One attempts to *didasko* or reveal his philosophy, morality, or pleasure as the supreme standard. British author and naturalist Charles Darwin wrote, "Ignorance more frequently begets confidence than does knowledge." Such confidence in one's self comes from knowledge. (This knowledge is either perceived or credible.) And because self-knowledge is always seen as subjective truth, ignorance has a very broad definition.

There are two antidotes for self-righteousness. The first of these is guilt. Guilt is the frequent or primary indicator to mankind that his own righteousness (whether through knowledge, philosophy, or religion) cannot be sustained.

This fact is why hedonists are the least self-righteous of the three classes of men. In order that passions in the fulfilling thereof always causes guilt of conscience at the preliminary stage. This occurs because for one of three possible reasons. The first reason is that concupiscence is always followed by mental intercourse and evaluation. Once an individual weighs their actions, positively and negatively, guilt is induced.

The second reason is that usually inordinate actions are executed upon the weaker vessel. (This is viewed from the male standpoint, but is not limited to this sex.) Physical coercion, deceit, dishonesty, and bribery are greatly evident in such actions. It is here that the same self-dialogue now examines the grief afflicted upon the object of lust. The greater the coercion, whether physical or mental or emotional, leads to the greater likelihood that guilt will be present in the sub-conscious of man.

And finally, the fervent pursuit of pleasure can have a direct effect upon the social health of the individual. Lasciviousness has no restraint. Therefore, it can invade and contaminate every aspect of one's essence. When this imbalance manifests itself, it, again, is able to negatively protrude mind and consciousness.

In the hedonist, guilt plays no motivating factor in curbing actions. The desire for pleasure in this group is so unrelenting that it can be constrained only by continual intervention. When intervention is not administered, the desire overrides guilt, which, in turn, creates a *specific conversation.* This is a continual practice which openly or covertly becomes the center or definition of one's existence.

Through continued practice, the guilt that comes from hedonism slowly modifies itself and becomes what is known as anti-guilt. To suppress the conviction of conscience, the individual's subconscious begins suppressing conviction by psychological recalibration, which then justifies the actions committed. One begins, in effect, to take pleasure in pleasure regardless of consequences. This is evidenced by the deep infatuation of the act.

Guilt also plays a major role in the religious. This is because in most religions, righteousness is said to be earned and not imputed. If righteousness is earned, then it is altogether self-righteous in works and appearance. So what happens when self-righteous acts are not fulfilled contrary to the prescribed standards? The result is guilt. In religion, though, guilt has a procedure to be reconciled. This is why at times religion can be the greatest elixir for guilt.

By the same token, guilt in religion can also be very detrimental. There are many religions that command self-harm, degradation, or other similar destructive displays of asceticism, in order to atone for guilt.

The second antidote for self-righteousness is tragedy and sorrow. Tragedy is the reminder to mankind that no matter how righteous you are in your conceits, circumstances cannot be completely controlled. The whole motive for self-righteousness is an attempt to worship. The byproduct of tragedy is the perception that worship has not been accomplished.

What Is Gained

What is gained in this thing we call life? Does it really matter what type of person we are, and does it matter what type of life we live? Is there truly such thing as a healthy existence? And what is the meaning?

From the standpoint of philosophy, the answers to all of these questions are all subjective at best. The great thinker and philosopher Sigmund Freud wrote that the meaning of life was to love and work. His conclusion seems simplistically profound on the surface. But upon closer evaluation, one can only ponder what the statement truly means. "What is one to work for? Whom is one to love? And can one work for love?" These are just a few of the questions that can be inquired of this theory. And when one factors in the distinct types of individuals with their hierarchy of needs, we encounter a homeostatic algorithm that leaves us none the better and none the worse.

It is that this point in my writing that I will begin to offer my hypothesis as to what is gained in this thing called life. I dare not call this a new philosophy. What I hope to inspire is the truth that revelation of oneself (besides that from divine or intellectual means) comes truly from suffering.

There exist three classes of suffering to which an individual can endure. The first of these is consequential. This is suffering that is a cause-and-effect result based upon a personal choice. Some examples of these are diseases, addiction, incarceration, and poverty. A direct trigger of an act such as lawlessness creates the possibility of incarceration. Slothfulness can easily beget poverty, which, in turn, produces the consequence of the specific suffering.

The second is inflicted suffering as a result of social triggers. This type reveals itself in the greatest possible ways. What society might call "moral evils" plays the greatest factor in this type. When ethical decisions are perverted (ethical either in the realm or revelation or philosophy—and all ethics must come from either or the two), natural stimuli then evolve into inflicted suffering. (This reality is greatly based upon other variables such as geography, culture, and government.)

Lastly, we have what is known as divine or natural suffering. This suffering can be the similar or, in fact, the same occurrences as those in the two previous groups. What separates natural suffering is that it appears random. Therefore, this type is the most difficult to endure overcome in a positive sense. Examples of natural suffering are natural disasters or un-acquired diseases.

It is no contradiction that suffering occurs regardless of a person's type. This because all classes of people endure the same suffering. This is most evident in natural suffering, which is independent of actions or beliefs. This is also revealed by inflicted social suffering which degenerates entire communities. And while it would seem that consequential suffering would be distinct, since it is based on actions, it actually is not, because we all share the same needs. So, in essence, all mankind is linked by the two single threads of need and suffering.

All inflicted consequential suffering derives from the inability to properly fulfill the three basic needs. When a man's needs are not made in the ordained manner then perversion will take place. This, in turn, produces suffering on one or more levels. It should be obvious that when one does not eat, he suffers hunger. Hunger is an evidence that all is not well in the natural order.

The lack of fulfillment of the underlying intrinsic needs is an even greater suffering. (I say greater based on the assumption that emotional and mental anguish far exceeds that of its physical counterpart.) A lack of perceived acceptance or love produces loneliness and separation anxiety. A lack of societal intercourse leads to feelings of worthlessness. And a perversion of worship can produce some of the most profound suffering. It has been stated in philosophy that more atrocities have been done in the name of religion than in any other thing. It is difficult to disagree with that notion.

Aspiration

English philosopher Bertrand Russell said, "There are three simple but overwhelmingly strong passions that govern my life, these are the longing for love, the search for knowledge, and the unbearable pity for the suffering of mankind." Mr. Russell's quote perfectly reveals man's aspiration, which is hope. Out of the darkness of suffering, mankind has the uncanny knack to aspire. And in this hope, the three desires Russell invokes, are so reinstated by the mankind's intrinsic desires that they serve as the blueprint for everything good in the human being.

I attempt to offer at anti-thesis to Mr. Russell. In doing so, I hope to reveal a more perspicuous view of aspiration. "*One cannot truly love until he is experienced hatred, knowledge cannot be obtained until ignorance is a field, and pity for the suffering cannot be manifest, unless one has suffered himself.*"

All desires are intensified (not engaged) by their polar opposites. A man's religious desire for holiness is provoked by the appearance of depravity either outside or inside of himself. The philosopher's quest for wisdom is and is fueled by the lack thereof. And the hedonist has his desire for pleasure fueled or motivated by his seeking for an escape from pain. Because aspiration is inspired through suffering, the greater the suffering means the greater the aspiration can be.

So, what is the individual aspiration of mankind? Ask yourself that question: those of you who or aspiring for what you aspire for. But the answer is likely derived from your deepest suffering. It is at this point that it is important to remember that aspiration is not independent of the three basic needs. In effect, aspiration is the triggering of a specific need caused by the suffering of the lack. For example, the natural desire for worship becomes *a priori* when vanity or worthlessness is experienced. Therefore, the individual aspires for religious freedom.

Another question is: "do all men have aspiration?" The answer is a surprising "no". This is because since desolation, being the immediate byproduct of suffering (and desolation the absolute subjection to vanity), aspiration could then be essential strangled and made desolate. Desolation is able to subdue all things into it (including hope). In these instances, aspiration is not found.

You may then ask, "What creates the difference between the one who aspires and the one that remains desolate?" On the most common level, some ascribed this occurrence to the thing called *fate*. It was the Roman poet Horace who said, "*Drop the question what tomorrow may bring, and count as profit every day that fate allows you.*" Some philosophers and scientists proclaim genetics as the overriding factor in this determination. Others name variables such as experience, culture, and opportunity as the means. (And an example of such is a young man who desires freedom for his country, because his native land is at war.) And on the far right of the spectrum, there are those who hold the belief of a divinely ordered system of predestination, which determines the roles of men.

It should be obvious to the psyche of man that that the world, in its most basic elements, suggests a divine ordination. It would foolish and outright ignorant to think otherwise. Just looking at the human cell gives us a glimpse of an organ that is far more complex than any celestial galaxy our eyes could have ever beheld. Speaking of eyes, each one with 120,000,000 rods sales can process information faster than any existing supercomputer. The 10 to the 13th power number of cells that comprise the human body all derive from one solitary cell. And the great scientific mystery is how from one cell, over 200 different types reveal themselves each having a unique and specific role. The human genome (if uncoiled) would be a written page of information extending from the earth to the sun and 70 times beyond. The DNA strand appears as a ladder ascending to a height we know not of. It would be inexplicable to believe that random chaos is the cord that holds all things together. Therefore, aspiration is not based on chance; it is based on an act of the will. The question is then posed: whose will?

The Formation of Character

The condensed definition of the word "character" is a certificate of qualities. This is a very meaningless definition. True character (in the positive sense alone) is the girth of a man. Apart from intellect and reason, it is that thing that separates him from the bottom echelon of man; even distinguishing humanity from animality. The character of a man defines one's purpose for doing, believing, and being.

There are five main stimuli that are required in the formation of character. These are morality, patience, experience, hope, and the knowledge of suffering. Without any one of these things, character is only defined by non-essential standards and visible external behavior. But when and if a man habitually practices and embodies these marks while exerting these qualities, we can be sure virtuous character is present.

The formation of character is altogether more commonly found in the religious type. There are two specific reasons for this. The first is that religion adheres to the belief of divine revelation, which commands submission to a moral law. Depending on the practice, when such a law is followed, a sense of morality is supplanted or imputed.

The desire for worship, when fulfilled by either self-righteousness or some deity, is the greatest cause of morality in man. Even the man that does not subscribe to the belief of absolute revelation will subconsciously display a form of morality to satisfy that desire to worship.

The second reason for character in this type is because, second to race and gender, distinct religion is the most intolerant attribute of mankind. Simply stated, religious intolerance and persecution have almost the greatest ability to produce character. This is the product of one (supposedly) having divine motivation to endure trials, and to aspire, as one suffers for the hope which he practices.

While race is the most intolerant attribute, racial discrimination is less likely to produce the grandiose character that comes from religious persecution. Consequential suffering is always more likely to produce character than is inflicted suffering. Suffering by choice is obviously more rationalized than suffering without choice.

The formation of character is by no means impossible, but, as discussed, is less evidently found in the philosopher. The reason is that philosophy is always in a state of constant change, seeking to define the evolving world around itself. The philosopher is more prone to analyze affliction than to respond to or to endure it. In philosophy, empirical knowledge is delegated to the lower realm, while hope is always seen as a defense mechanism.

(A side note on philosophy is that morality in philosophy is not necessary for enlightenment. This, in essence, gives the philosopher the prerogative to become his own moral law.)

Finally, the discussion of character in the hedonist must be addressed. The discussion will be brief because the virtue of character cannot fully exist in such a one. As discussed previously, if any one of the five products of character is removed, then one can have no negotiable character present. Hedonism can negatively be described as the lack of morality. Therefore, no man of character can be a devout hedonist.

What Is Victory?

With all that has been discussed so far, what have we learned? Hopefully we have gleaned much. But up to this point, there's been no definite prescription for how one gains victory in this thing called *life*.

It should be obvious by now that the true balance is derived from properly fulfilling the three basic regardless of what type of person we currently find ourselves to be. In doing so, we are able to see that hedonism is more draining than it is nourishing and that philosophy is always interpreted by circumstance. And with natural and afflicted suffering always present, philosophy simply cannot sustain itself. In religion, we discover that only one can be true. This leaves a majority of the devout deceived.

Let us, therefore, conduct a cognitive experiment. Beginning with the hedonist, let us examine the best possible outcome for each type. Let us imagine that this man has every possible pleasure in his grasp. It is also assumed that he is immune to any law that prohibits him from engaging in deviancy. He has free range to do whatever he wants, with whomever he wants, whenever he wants. What will such a life amount to? The answer is complete and utter depredation. As the carnal body begins to age and weaken, the hedonist is left with unfulfilled mental and physical desires. His needs only cause internal suffering and pain, which, in turn, only further fuel his hedonism. (It is similar to an aged man with severe arthritis reaching his arm for his pain medicine. The more he reaches the more pain it causes.) This will be a circle of suffering that has no end.

Now take the great philosopher. Imagine that his perceived wisdom crosses all borders and boundaries. Such a wise man is revered by almost all, because of his knowledge and dogma. It was seen that his philosophy is dogmatic, because of the overwhelming response by those who adhere to it. Consider that knowledge helping, assisting, and uplifting society in new ways, as it serves as a tool that meets the needs of fellow man. What sense of satisfaction would be begotten from begetting such wisdom?

But even this thing is flawed. As great as such a philosophy could be, suffering still continues, millions go impoverished, injustice still reigns, discrimination abounds, and diseases spread. The greatest of man's imaginations are unable to inaugurate the social and domestic utopia that we all truly seek. (*George Bernard Shaw, H.G. Wells, and the Flavian Society do well to prove this point.*) There would be needed a true *form* of philosophy to form a system of unity that could deal with the diversity of all the world's ever changing ills. Therefore, philosophy serves only as dampened gauze to a weak, wounded, and dying world.

Now, let us consider the religious. His life is filled with good works and morality. He also displays a profound patience even in the great trials, though it is in the next life for which the man's hope is found. Death serves a bypass that ushers in the revelation of his maker. He is given the promise and reward that so exceeds imagination that no mere words would be adequate for description.

This man could also find himself deceived. How terrible would it be to realize that what he has believed his entire life is nothing more than charade? It would be either by ignorance or a deceptive lie that one's existence would either culminate to absolute annihilation or absolute wrath by an angry deity. Or at best, religion would be a waste of life, which could have been spent in the matrix of pleasure or in pursuit of *sophistry*.

My conclusion is that it should be the aspiration of all mankind to become religious. And seeing that only one religion can be true, it should be noted that the religion I suggest is that of Christianity. While religion does not always provide specific answers as to why we suffer individually, (although the answer is provided for universal suffering), it does give the promise to those seeking, the hope of something grandiose and eternal.

Therefore, Charles, the only reasonable and rational worldview is a religious one. Anything real and radical must be revealed. And the nature of revelation itself points to the form and ideal of a personal Revealer.

J.J.

To Be Continued...

Appendix A
The Lost Letters of Cornelius Van Til to C.S. Lewis: The Use of Presuppositions in Lewis' Book *Miracles*.

The following fictional conversation was written for a Master's Level C.S. Lewis apologetics class at Westminster Theological Seminary. After joining the class five weeks late, I was left with no other topic to dissect than that the use of presuppositions in the works of C.S. Lewis's book *Miracles*. It was a daunting task, but I remember that Dr. Scott Oliphint once described how the father of presuppositional apologetics, Cornelius Van Til, once wrote C.S. Lewis concerning some of his writings. While Van Til was not a staunch critic of Lewis, he did have his qualms about much of Lewis' theology.

In writing these fictional letters, my attempt was to imitate both men's style as closely I possibly could. This was easier for me, because I had been a lifelong Lewis fan could somewhat imitate his manner of prose and wit. Concerning Van Til, I needed to dive head long into more of his writing to discover his line of thought and how it ran contra-parallel to that of Lewis'. I also sought to season the work with enough British and Dutch axioms as to make the work believable, but not be blatant in my attempt to engender authenticity.

The result is a candid view of the use of presuppositions in the apologetics of these two men. Filled with humor, quips, and quotes from both men's works, I hope to have done justice to both of these literary and academic giants.

The Lost Letters of Cornelius Van Til to C.S. Lewis: The Role of Presupposition in Apologetics

September 13, 1951

Dear Professor Lewis,

I do confess I consider it a pleasure to have the opportunity to write you. I have heard all too well that you are extremely cordial when it applies to reading the letters of your inquirers. I hope that this letters finds you well, and well at work at what I'm sure will be another best-seller.

The words of this letter are written in regards to your latest book, *Miracles*. It was recently brought to my attention by a student here at the campus of Westminster where I teach that you use common presuppositions in the form of the cumulative argument. You may not know this, but I myself have been labeled the modern revivalist of presuppositional apologetics. I personally never really liked the terminology of presuppositional apologetics, preferring preeminent apologetics—simply holding the Bible as preeminent criteria for *apologia*. This is in distinction from the classical or evidential methodologies that we have seen since the time of Aquinas or the cumulative mode in which you have given rise to. But, as all arguments must commence with some form of presupposition, I, then, embrace the idea for the mere sake of engaging my opponents in the argument that neutral ground cannot exist when the agnostic, atheist, or heterodox philosopher denies the reality of the Christian worldview.

After reading the first half of your work *Miracles*, I do concur that I am seeing some logical discrepancies with your use of presupposition, as it relates to our shared Christian faith. If I may simply and briefly dissect the first chapter of the book, I believe my point will be made. And please remember, I write with the sincerest of sentiments.

In the first chapter, you immediately supplant the priority of pure *scriptura revelatio* for philosophical inquiry. Similar to the loathsome classical method, you (without using causal arguments) still fall into the snare of Romanism by believing - or at least implying that there exists the common ground of philosophic reasoning that would even allow your unbelieving reader to determine the veracity and validity of the miraculous. In my view, this point of contact that you assert is really no point of contact at all. When you state:

"If they (miracles) are impossible, then no amount of historical evidence will convince us. If they are possible but immensely improbable, then only mathematically demonstrative evidence will convince us: and since history never provides that degree of evidence for any event, history can never convince us that a miracle occurred. If, on the other hand, miracles are not intrinsically improbable, then the existing evidence will be sufficient to convince us that quite a number of miracles have occurred. The result of our historical enquires thus depends on the philosophical views which we have been holding before we begin to look at the evidence. The philosophical question must therefore come first."[1]

This presupposition of philosophical inquiry cannot be the *a priori* or neutral ground from which the Christian apologist must engage his opponent. When traveling with the your opponent, you do not first travel in the same direction and in the same automobile with the natural man for some distance in order to mildly suggest to the driver that they ought perhaps to change their course somewhat and follow a road that goes at a different slant from the one they are on. There is but one way to the truth. The natural man is travelling on it, but in the wrong direction.[2]

As I have previously written concerning your other works, *Beyond Personality* and *The Abolition of Man*, you seek for objective standards in ethics, in literature, and in life everywhere. But you

---

[1] C. S. Lewis, *Miracles.* New York, New York: Macmillian, 1947, 3

[2] Cornelius Van Til, *Defense of the Faith.* Phillipsburg, New Jersey: P&R Publishing, 1955, 113

hold that objectivity may be found in many places. You speak of a general objectively that is common between Christians and non-Christians, but surely this general objectivity is found in a formal sense only. To say that there is or must be an objective standard is not the same as to say what that standard is. And it is the *what* that is all important.[3]

Feel free to respond in kind at your earliest convenience.

Sincerely,
Dr. Cornelius Van Til
Professor of Apologetics
Westminster Seminary

[3] Ibid., 82

Dear Dr. Van Til,

Thank you for your kind letter dated the Thirteenth of September. While I do confess that your letter was the first time I have heard of you, after a little research, I now understand your prominence and prestige in the traditions of Dutch reformed theology. It is a pleasure.

I am delighted to see that you would respond to me with such assistance as to the area of "presuppositional argumentation." You may well know (as I confess in most of my books) that I am only a layman, not theologically trained in the more concise studies of biblical or systematic theology. You, as a professor of such divine truths, have the privilege of dispensing the full monty while I—playing my hand at incognito—have to be box clever: making myself a Christian flanker in a rugby game dominated by naturalist fullbacks.

Well, let me expound my reasoning for this particular presupposition that you inquire of. I can assume from the brief study that I have done of your works in apologetics, that you would much rather have me refer, not essentially to the issue of probability or possibility of miracles, as I do in my work, but to your bequeathed system which finds preeminent the issue of epistemology. In your method, I should immediately show how Christianity takes precedence over every opposing view by the means of *redutio ad absurdum*. If I only I was taught at Princeton in the time of the theological giants such as yourself, Machen, and Warfield... but it was not the case.

You find some fault in my method of the initial injection the Carneades assertion of probability/possibility. Well, I would certainty be open to an alternative formula. But honestly, in my own assessment, this is how the common folk and even the practical materialist reason. Therefore, I seek to avouch how one's presupposition concerning miracles (almost entirely based on the probability possibility argument) must first be ascertained before the controversy can be driven any further. Thus, the goal of this work is to candidly foster a probable presupposition concerning the phenomena of miracles, not to prove it. Because of this, I do believe that the philosophical proof must precede the epistemological before evident progress can be made.

Moving on with the work, I sought to maintain as parallel as possible the theo-philosophical definitions when characterizing the terms: Miracle— an interference with nature by supernatural power[4], Naturalist—one who believes that nothing but nature exists[5], and Supernaturalist—one who believes that there exists something in addition to nature that is outside of nature.[6]

The common objection to these labels is concerning their generality—that they (as some argue) enable me to construct a straw-man argument. To this, I disagree. When I state that, "If naturalism is true (the view that all things exist in the framework of nature with nature itself being *a se*), then we do know in advance that miracles are impossible: nothing can come into nature from the outside because there is nothing to come in, Nature being everything,"[7] my detractors often accuse me of attributing to my ascription of naturalism some type of concealed determinism—the view that every event (except the first one) has antecedent causes sufficient for its occurrence. But concerning these detractors, I must wipe the floor with such a rebuttal. Those who accuse me of implying determinism truly have placed themselves in a sticky wicket. For they who seek to find a middle ground between naturalism and supernaturalism surely cannot. It is similar to a blind man asking his wife to light a candle after a power outage. Every naturist is a determinist and has already (by voluntary volition) closed his eyes to the possibility of anything outside of his material view, and not even dualism can give him a conceivable way out.

[4] C.S. Lewis, *Miracles*, 2,3
[5] Ibid.
[6] Ibid.
[7] Ibid., 10

I've written too much for now. Dr. Van Til, please inform me as to whether my reply was sufficient in explanation. And if not, I look forward to your next letter.

C. S. Lewis.

Dear Professor Lewis,

I can truly see that we will at this current juncture differ greatly concerning the presupposition of neutral ground. You view it as a necessary starting place in which you engage your opponent though you do not adequately confront your reader as to how they are able to have "view" at all. To me, the idea of "neutrality" is simply a colorless suit that covers a negative attitude toward God. In truth, every fact in this world, the God of the Bible claims, has his stamp indelibly engraved upon it. How then could you be neutral with respect to such a God? It is like a citizen of the United States taking a stroll through the crowds in Washington on the Fourth of July and wondering whether the Lincoln Memorial belongs to anyone.[8] But for now on this issue I rest my case.

I shall move on to the more positive critique of chapters 3-5. In these sections, you cover the topics of: "Naturalism Ruling Out Reason," "The Interconnection of Reason to Nature," "The Extraction of Morality from Reason." (Worry not, Professor Lewis; I shall be brief. I have to teach systematic theology in less than an hour. We will be discussing the transcendental argument for God. Would you like a syllabus?)

Concerning the interconnection of reason to nature, you state in the chapter "The Cardinal Difficulty of Naturalism" that "All possible knowledge, then, depends on the validity of reasoning."[9] The implied premise of such a conclusion is found in your idea that the knowledge we have of all information is that of "observation plus inference" as it relates to nature. While the logical deduction you pose is certainly viable, I question whether such a deduction best fits into a whole and fully developed epistemological argument. It does seem a bit truncated, wouldn't you say? While your Ground Consequent Argument (the

---

[8] C.V. Til, *Why I Believe in God.* Philadelphia, Pennsylvania: Great Commission Publications, 1948, 5

[9] C.S. Lewis, *Miracles*, 14

mathematical logistic of finding the *reason* behind the *cause*) enables you to show the biological absurdity of the unbeliever's lack of account for his own accounting, I still believe that you are remaining too long in the neutral corner of the ring with your opponent. As I have stated before and now state again, the natural man must be blasted out of his hideouts... the reformed apologist throws down the gauntlet and challenges his opponent to a duel of life and death from the start.[10]

The reality that I believe you and many semi-classical/cumulative apologists miss is that reason in itself has a metaphysical endowment. For truly as you state, if reason is the ultimate criteria for observing objective truth, what canon is there to distinguish how reasoning must be nothing more than one link in a causal chain which stretches back to the beginning and forward to the end of time?[11] The metaphysical link is found in this: it takes something we Christians call "faith" to even consider reason valid. There exists the absolute necessity of "faith" to believe that my reason is interpreting "facts" correctly. And if the unbeliever exercises faith and does not admit to it, he is using what we refer to here at Westminster as *borrowed capital*. He has no right to believe or assert truth in terms of his own presuppositions, but only in terms of Christian ones.[12] It is here that you have your opponent in a "sticky wicket," as referred to in your last letter. If you have him trapped there, keep him there and slay him without delay. This is your privilege as a Christian apologist.

When you speak of the interconnection between reason and nature in chapter 4, I see much positive material here, especially in your categorization of nature and supernature. It is a valid judgment when you state, "Each (reason and human minds) has come into Nature from Supernature: each has it's taproot in an

---

[10] C.V. Til, *Defense of the Faith*, page 130

[11] C.S. Lewis, *Miracles*, 24

[12] Johns Frame, IIIM Magazine Online, Volume 2, Number 35, August 28 to September 3, 2000.

eternal, self-existent, rational Being, whom we call God."[13] I would definitely applaud you at this point as you show that there is an All-Conditioner who is able to communicate to reason and through reason.

Yet, proceeding from this point, you make a dastardly and unexpected error. You write, "Nature is quite powerless to produce a rational thought."[14] This does not presuppose the means of God's general revelation as I am sure you know. Now while I am very familiar with the similarity of your use of Natural Law or the *Tao* with what we theologians label "general revelation," your vagueness does not do justice to your supposed system of supernature and how it invades nature. Natural revelation (including moral law and the created world) shows that natural revelation is, even after the fall, perspicuous in character.[15] The perspicuity of God's revelation in nature depends for its very meaning upon the fact that it is an aspect of the total and a totally voluntary revelation of a God who is self-contained."[16] Scripture also plainly reveals these truths as St. Paul argues:

"Because that which may be known of God is manifest in them; for God hath shewed it unto them. For the invisible things of him from the creation of the world are clearly seen, being understood by the things that are made, even his eternal power and Godhead; so that they are without excuse." (Romans 1:19-20)

Herein lies a great attestation of God manifesting himself through the medium of nature by the instrumentation of reason. This is what we might call "Presuppositional Dianetics." God presupposes that despite the noetic effect of sin, that mankind still has the reason to reason that God is the ultimate reason behind all

[13] C.S. Lewis, *Miracles*, 26
[14] Ibid., 28
[15] C.V. Til, Defense of the Faith 120
[16] C.V. Til, *The Infallible Word*, 259

things reasonable. And if God presupposes it, let us, then, both suppose it to be true.

Sincerely, C.V.T.

Dear Dr. Van Til

Thanks for your letter dated March 18. As far as not having sufficient "relative" time to address the issue in chapter 5, don't bother. The issues in that section were all relative anyway.

Concerning our topic of presupposition, it seems to me that we are not galaxies apart as it may appear. I believe that by the 5th and 6th chapters, I might be able to show you this. We both know all too well how the naturalists say that morality is just a product of societal conditioning. It's like when King and Ketley place the phrase "The waterfall is sublime" in their pretentious similitude of a grammar book not meant to teach the critical apparatus of language and its usage, but to insert a pseudo-philosophy that sets to assert a subjective view of values which attributes nothing as objectively good or evil. But what I desired to reveal from such fallacy is that if natural law; the *ought* and *ought not,* were explained by irrational or non-moral materialism, then those ideas are pure illusions.[17] I believe that this is further revealed by the likes of world's H.G. Wells, who on one side of the coin, say that all moral judgments are apparitions, but yet on the other, you find them exhorting the masses to work for posterity, to promote education, and to live and die for the good of the human race.[18] This reality plainly suggests to me that naturalists do not truly act according to what they propose to presuppose.

In the 6th chapter, my whole point (which I believe you will or have already seen) is this: that the naturalist has and is engaged in thinking about nature, but has not attended to the fact that they were thinking.[19] This is consistent with your previous statement, "The unbeliever does not account for his own accounting." I think the only difference we have on this subject is that of semantics. I say that reason is done through the medium of the brain, as vision

[17] C.S. Lewis, *Miracles*, 5
[18] Ibid., 36
[19] Ibid., 41

of a garden might take place through the medium of a window. You, I assume, would refer to this as a limiting concept, in the Christian sense[20], unable to be truly realized apart from the grace of special revelation. So, in the relation to miracles, God reveals the general character of nature for the very purpose of manifesting his special revelation through it.

It is in the next chapter that I begin to deal with the chronological snobbery of many materialists of our day. The common thought of late modernity, is that the acceptance of miracles, as told to us by biblical revelation, is simply a primitive and archaic belief based not on any true evidential proof, but on ignorance and the sad disposition of living before the enlightenment.

Miracles certainly do carry with it the connotation of red herrings to our so-called reasonable minds. When we suggest that something outside nature has invaded nature, increasing our knowledge of nature does not make it more credible.[21] Therefore, a virgin birth is still incredibly contrary to reason whether you are a 1st-century Palestinian mid-wife or a 20th-century gynecologist. Man's ever expanding knowledge is not the presupposition for understanding natural law, but only the *a posteri* from which we do understand. Thus, miracles not only invade natural law (making themselves utterly supra-natural), but simultaneously invade our reason as well.

In closing, Dr. Van Til, presuppositions play a major role in my argument for the supernatural. My method seeks to reveal how all mankind has the same presuppositions for truth, just buried under strongholds or error. As you said in a previous letter, we are all on the same road of truth, some are just walking in the wrong direction.

---

[20] C.V. Til, *Introduction to Systematic Theology*. Phillipsburg, New Jersey: P&R Publishing, 2007, 68

[21] C.S. Lewis, *Miracles*, 48

The major presupposition for the supernatural is found in chapter 11. After clearing the road of the Horrid Little Red things (the hindrance of language in the understanding of miracles), it is manifest by and through natural law or common grace as the Reformed say, that there exists a God. But the question then evolves into, "What type of God is it that exists?" (This is where the theologian is able to be much more dogmatic than I.) But in my estimation, both the transcendental God and the pantheistic God emerge as the clear contenders for deity. The arguments for pantheism, as Spinoza and Hegel would like us to believe, are many. I need not go into at this point. But the case for it must be disposed of by the "Presuppositional Dianetic," as you might refer to. Mankind has the reason to perceive that, because the created order is concrete and individual, so, too, must be he who created it. The words of a poem do not simply derive from the presence of metre. There must be a poet to place the words within.

It is like what I told a materialist philosopher during my visit to Cambridge for a debate: "Your views do not seem to line up with who you are. And when I say who you are, I don't mean, your character, upbringing, or genealogy, I mean who you are as a rational and orderly man. If you say that chance has given life to all things we know, then the product looks nothing like the source. What I mean is this; if random chaos is your maker and originator; then how come you stand before me as an orderly being? Your words are not chaotic; (sometimes incredulous but still intelligible.) The way you walk and move shows order and fluidity (although philosophically you're on a slippery slope.). The very make-up of your body and circulatory system give evidence to a unique working program. What I'm saying is that your physical make up has no evidence of random chaos and mere naturalism. You would have an argument if spontaneous human combustion was the means of procreation, but it is not."

It has been a pleasure, Dr. Van Til.

C. S. Lewis.

Appendix B
Paul Meets Mohammed: The Apostle and the Prophet

'Paul Meets Mohammed' is a fictional apologetic relating to the life of Paul of Tarsus and Mohammed of Mecca. My goal is to contrast two of the greatest names and influences in religious history. The story takes place in 7th Century Arabia and happens upon a chance meeting between the two men. Neither one immediately knows the identity of the other when they begin to engage in a discourse on faith. While the plot and storyline are fictional, many of the historical places and events recalled are factual.

Using actual words from the New Testament and the Koran, "Paul Meets Mohammad" is my idea of what a conversation would sound like between two men who represent such contrasting ideas about culture, religion, and God. The great chasm between their faiths is clearly displayed. I sought to be as unbiased as possible, allowing readers to decide for themselves which arguments are valid or fallacious.

Much research went into this story. My study of the Koran, Hadiths, and Arabic tradition were essential in helping to depict a realistic view of ancient Islam and of its Messenger. I am also thankful for the Muslim acquaintances who were kind enough to help me along the path of writing this work.

I decided to include a short introduction and synopsis of New Testament and Koranic literary criticism and intertexuality.[22] I believe this concise aid will be important in helping the reader understand the underlying rigidness of Islamic scholars that prevent a true and succinct textual criticism on the Koran. It will also aid the layman in seeing that at the core of the dispute between Islam and Christianity, the inspiration and authenticity of both holy texts is questioned.

[22] "Intertextuality," http://dictionary.reference.com/browse/intertextuality (accessed August 10, 2010).

My goal for writing this short story is to display a creative but accurate inquiry into the comparison of the world's two largest religions. I have an unrelenting passion for all men to know the Truth. I hope that all who read this work will be enlightened to that end.

Text Criticism and Intertexuality of the New Testament and Koran

Introduction

The New Testament and the Koran serve as the divinely inspired, authoritative written texts for nearly half of the world's population. Christians and Muslims look to these two texts as divine revelation disclosed by God for the sake of knowing and following God's will. While both documents have the self attestation of divine origin, both were transmitted through human authors. It is therefore proper that the science of textual criticism be applied to these literary works. Sound textual criticism allows scholars to discover the textual errors, variances, and original readings of the text. In this work, I will seek to show by research the comparative criticisms of the New Testament and the Koran.

History of the New Testament

There is much to be discussed when studying the formation of the New Testament canon in the history of the early church, but there are a few preliminary and general statements that should be made. Early Christians believed that God instituted a new age with the incarnation of Jesus Christ. This incarnation was followed by the redemptive-historical act of his death and resurrection, which made the possibility of salvation from sin a reality. Jesus' followers saw this work as being the fulfillment of God's promises to the Jewish people while simultaneously ushering in a New Covenant, which God promised to the Old Testament Prophets such as David, Ezekiel, and Jeremiah. (Jeremiah 31:31)

Some see the New Testament writings as the interpretation of the divine act. If it were true that God had personally intervened in history for the purpose of redemption, then naturally oral or written tradition would be necessary to rightly understand that work. This seems to be in line with the words of Christ to his disciples in John 15:26-27: "But when the Comforter is come, whom I will send unto you from the Father, even the Spirit of truth, which proceedeth from the Father, he shall testify of me: And ye also shall bear witness, because ye have been with me from the beginning."[23] It is therefore from the Apostles of Christ that a divinely organic outgrowth of authority and inspiration began to manifest in written form.

Three literary forms appear in the New Testament. These forms are narrative, prophecy, and letter (epistle), with the majority being in the form of the letter. These epistles taught doctrine while exhorting believers in the practical areas of Christian life. These letters were recopied and circulated throughout the Christian community as authoritative. The apostle Paul writes, "And when this epistle is read among you, cause that it be read also in the church of the Laodiceans; and that ye likewise read the epistle from Laodicea." (Colossians 4:16)

Due to the military conquests of Alexander the Great and the spread of Greek culture, Greek became the most common language throughout Asia Minor and the Roman Empire. Almost all of the text of the New Testament was written in this common language, Koine Greek. This made for greater circulation and understandability throughout the Gentile church, which constituted the majority of Christian believers. While papyrus and parchment were used in some of the writing, eventually the book form of Codex became popular and was widely used.

While many of the writings now regarded as the New Testament circulated throughout Asia Minor in the first century, it was not until the fourth century that Christians recognized a single body of writings as the New Testament. This body of writings was termed "canon." The word "canon" comes from the Greek word, *kanon* which literally means straight rod or measuring stick. In its common usage, the word represents the criteria or standard by which a thing is measured as true or normative. This word primarily became associated with the New

---

[23] *Holy Bible*, King James Version (public domain).

Testament by early church father Clement of Alexandria.[24] It is in the writings of Athanasius that we initially see all twenty-seven books mentioned in the category of Scripture.

History of the Koran

The writings of the Koran were introduced in the early 7th century by the Arabian Mohammed of Mecca. At the time, Mecca was saturated in religio-political idolatry that was centered at the temple Kaaba. The city was under control of the Quaryish, the dominant leading Arab tribal family. During this time, Mohammed, who was a Hanif (ancient Arab God-seeker) withdrew to Mt. Hira for reflection and contemplation. In the Arabic month of Ramadan, he claimed that he had been given special revelation by the angel Gabriel. These proclamations were to be the final revelation of God to mankind.

According to Koranic and Islamic tradition, Mohammed was illiterate, unable to read or write. However, he is commanded by Allah (Arabic for God) to proclaim his words while instituting Islam as the true and final religion.[25] These revelations supposedly continued for a period of 23 years and were compiled in codex form after Mohammed's death in 632 A.D.

The Koran includes a series of historical and religious utterances that detail the rise of Islam, short and intercut narratives from other literary sources, doctrinal and practical commands of the religion, and exhortations of preparation for the coming Islamic Theocracy. Concerning the historicity of the Koran, Patricia Crone states, "[T]he book is difficult to use as a historical source. The roots of this difficulty include unresolved questions about how it reached its classical form, and the fact that

[24] The word is translated "rule" in 1 Clement 7:2. W. K. Lowther Clarke, *The First Epistle of Clement to the Corinthians* (London: Society for Promoting Christian Knowledge; New York: The Macmillan Company, 1937), 52.

[25] Sura 96:2. Malik Ghulam Farid, ed., *The Holy Qur'an: Arabic Text and English Translation with Commentary* (London: The London Mosque, 1981), 1379.

it still is not available in a scholarly edition."[26]

The entire Koran was written in Arabic. The internal motivation for this is found in Sura 43:4, which states, "we have made it a book to be oft read and clear, eloquent language that you may understand."[27] Malik Ghulam Farid, Muslim scholar and editor, writes in his commentary, "(Arabic) conveys the sense of fulness [*sic*], abundance and clearness, and the Arabic language is so called because its roots are innumerable and are full of meanings and because it is most expressive, eloquent and comprehensive."[28]

It has been widely noted that there is a great lack of critical scholarship on the Koran. Most traditional records suggest that the Koran most likely was written using an amanuensis and dictated by Mohammed himself. The Koran was primarily a work that was recited and not written. Some forms of the Koran have been found to be written on stone, leather, or other natural materials. It was not until after the death of Mohammed that codification occurred. One of the earliest Caliphs (community leaders) of Islam was Abu Bakr. He was required by General Umar to correlate a codex of the Koran for the sake of preserving its legacy in the event of Muslim persecution or casualty. This led officially to the process of canonizing the text we now consider the Koran.

Intertextuality

The New Testament and the Koran differ greatly in the area of textuality (the nature of the text itself). The most basic difference is that of authorship. Contributing to the New Testament were at least six different authors from various locales, backgrounds, and cultures, while the Koran is ascribed to Mohammed alone. The textual form also varies. As stated earlier, the New Testament includes narrative, epistle, and prophecy,

---

[26] Patricia Crone, "What do we actually know about Mohammed?" June 10, 2008, http://www.opendemocracy.net/faith-europe_islam/mohammed_3866.jsp (accessed November 27, 2009).
[27] Farid, *The Holy Qur'an*, 1046.
[28] Farid, *The Holy Qur'an*, 483 (note 1357).

while the sayings of the Koran are in the forms of oracles or decrees.

Direct allusions to the Hebrew Scriptures are included in the Koranic literature. These constant references to the Hebrew faith have caused scholars to study how much of Judaism was borrowed and applied to the Koran. Jewish scholar Abraham Geiger was one of the first critics in comparative studies of the Bible and Koran. He sets forth the parameters in which his critical study is applied, stating:

> "Did Muhammad wish to borrow from Judaism? Could Muhammad borrow from Judaism? and if so, how was such borrowing possible for him? Was it compatible with his plan to borrow from Judaism? The second division must bring forward the facts to prove the borrowing, which has been stated on general grounds to have taken place. Only in this way can an individual proof of the kind referred to acquire scientific value, partly as throwing light upon the nature of Muhammad's plan, and partly as showing the intrinsic necessity of the fact and its actual importance by virtue of its connection with other facts of Muhammad's life and age."[29]

The Koran's Suras (chapters) do, at times, carry a type of crude literary poetry, having rhymes without a rhythmic or prosaic foundation. At times, there is much similarity to the Hebraic Scriptures in which the Prophets spoke in the name of the Lord. The Koran also uses unique imagery in portraying the declarations of Allah. Other parallels to the Jewish Torah and Prophets are found in its narrative forms. The Koran includes the names and/or personalities of at least seventy biblical figures. There are even detailed narratives, not found in the Old Testament, concerning patriarchal figures such as Joseph and

[29] Abraham Geiger, *Judaism and Islam*, trans. F. M. Young (1896), http://www.answering-islam.org/Books/Geiger/Judaism/sec11.htm, 2 (accessed August 11, 2010).

Abraham. The Koran, like the Pentateuch, promotes strict dietary laws that are necessary to please God and follow his commandments. Finally, Islam's Allah seems to possess the aura of the tribal deity that the God of ancient Judaism was regarded to possess.

While it is obvious that the New Testament cannot borrow from the Koran (having been written 6 centuries prior), there are numerous allusions to the Jewish Old Testament Scriptures. These allusions usually come in the form of fulfillment to the Old Testament texts. The book of Matthew is a prime example of this. There are at least 15 occasions in which the Greek verb *pleroo* (translated 'fulfilled') is used in connection with the Old Testament prophecies. Matthew 27:9 states, "Then was fulfilled that which was spoken by Jeremy the prophet, saying, And they took the thirty pieces of silver, the price of him that was valued, whom they of the children of Israel did value." Matthew, a disciple of Christ and an Orthodox Jew, would have been familiar with the Old Testament prophecies.

No epistle in the New Testament proclaims the Jewish-Christian relationship as the book of Hebrews. Written by an unknown author, this epistle seeks to relate the transcendence of Christ above the old Hebrew traditions. In the first chapter alone, the author quotes five Jewish Psalms for the purpose of showing the supremacy of Christ. Matthew Henry writes in his commentary, "The design of this epistle was to persuade and press the believing Hebrews to a constant adherence to the Christian faith, and perseverance and it..."[30]

There is a great disconnect in Islam regarding its relation to Christian and Hebrew texts. The Koran alludes to the divine origin of the New Testament Gospel (*Injil*) but never quotes or references it verbatim. There is also an indirect charge of textual corruption against Jews and Christians for perverting the words of

[30] Matthew Henry, *Commentary on the Whole Bible: Complete and Unabridged in One Volume* (Hendrickson, 2005) 2380.

the covenant. In Sura 5:14-15 Mohammed declares:

> "So, because of their breaking their covenant, We have cursed them and have hardened their hearts. They pervert the words from their proper places and have forgotten a good part of that with which they were exhorted....And from those also who say, 'We are Christians,' We took a covenant, but they too have forgotten a good part of that which they were exhorted."[31]

Historical Textual Criticism of the New Testament and Koran

From the early institution of the Christian Church, the *Parodosis*, or tradition passed down from the apostles, was considered authoritative and sufficient for doctrine and exhortation. With the pass of time, however, fewer eyewitnesses remained, which created a need for the sacred tradition to be recorded. These writings would be read and expounded upon in the local churches.

One of the earliest records of textual criticism of the New Testament was done by church father Irenaeus. While it is probable that textual criticism took place earlier, one of the earliest appearances occurs in the works of Irenaeus. Eldon J. Epp writes that Irenaeus favored a particular reading of Revelation 13:18 because it was "'found in all the good [or weighty] and ancient copies.'"[32] Other church father such as Origen and Jerome also referred to the various readings of New Testament texts.

The true source of New Testament textual criticism finds its roots in the human copyists who reproduced the sacred text. Textual critic Bruce Metzger writes, "In the early years of the Christian Church, marked by rapid expansion and consequent increased demand by individuals and by the congregations for copies of the Scriptures, the speedy multiplication of copies, even

[31] Farid, *The Holy Qur'an*, 246.

[32] Eldon J. Epp "Issues in New Testament Textual Criticism: Moving from the 19th Century to the 21st Century," in *Rethinking New Testament Textual Criticism*, ed. David A. Black (Grand Rapids, MI: Baker, 2002), 21.

by non-professional scribes, sometimes took precedence over strict accuracy of detail."[33] Therefore the goal of New Testament criticism, according to Metzger, is "to ascertain from the divergent copies which form of the text should be regarded as most nearly conforming to the original."[34]

Most of the information scholars possess concerning the formation of the Koran comes from the *hadiths*. These ancient writings contain narrative traditions that relate to the life of Mohammed and also the history and interpretation of Islam. Most Muslim scholars see these works as traditionally necessary for applying jurisprudence and doctrine as it relates the Koran.

The hadith *Sahih Bukhari* contains more historical information related to the Koran's canonization than any other book. Written in the 8th century by Muslim scholar, Muhammad Ibn Ismail al-Bukhari, it serves as a written record of Mohammed's prophetic traditions. Concerning the Koran and its dissemination through Islam's early leaders, it states, "Then the complete manuscripts (copy) of the Qur'an remained with Abu Bakr till he died, then with 'Umar till the end of his life, and then with Hafsa, the daughter of 'Umar."[35]

It was during the reign of Uthman Ibn Affan, the 3rd Caliph of Islam, that a great development took place in standardizing the Koran. In order to dissuade variations of the Koran from being recited and recopied, (there seems to have been evidence of this in Ancient Iraq) he organized a committee with the purpose of producing a unified and cohesive codex that would replace any variant texts. The Hadith states:

"Uthman then ordered Zaid bin Thabit, 'Abdullah bin

---

[33] Bruce M. Metzger, quoted in Paul D. Wegner, *A Student's Guide to Textual Criticism of the Bible: Its History, Methods & Results* (Downers Grove, IL: InterVarsity, 2006), 79.

[34] Bruce M. Metzger and Bart D. Ehrman, *The Text of the New Testament: Its Transmission, Corruption, and Restoration*, 4th ed. (New York: Oxford University Press, 2005), xv.

[35] Hadith of Sahih Bukhari, Volume 6, Book 61, Number 509, trans. M. Muhsin Khan, http://www.usc.edu/schools/college/crcc/engagement/resources/texts/muslim/hadith/bukhari/061.sbt.html (accessed August 12, 2010).

> AzZubair, Said bin Al-As and 'AbdurRahman bin Harith bin Hisham to rewrite the manuscripts in perfect copies.'Uthman said to the three Quraishi men, "In case you disagree with Zaid bin Thabit on any point in the Qur'an, then write it in the dialect of Quraish, the Qur'an was revealed in their tongue." They did so, and when they had written many copies, 'Uthman returned the original manuscripts to Hafsa. 'Uthman sent to every Muslim province one copy of what they had copied, and ordered that all the other Qur'anic materials, whether written in fragmentary manuscripts or whole copies, be burnt."[36]

The actions of Uthman have been a subject of great debate in the Islamic scholarly quarters. Many Muslims presuppose that the Koran has always been a unified Codex with no variants, but the history of Uthman's decree seems to suggest otherwise. If the variances in the text were those of simple grammar, there would probably be no need to order the destruction of prior texts (seeing that the Koran was mostly recited and not read). The drastic action by the Caliph shows that there were greater variances (possibly doctrinally) that Uthman did not want to survive.

It is unknown today how many ancient manuscripts of the Koran actually exist. One reason for this could be the motivation to conceal the great number of variances in the text of the Koran. Some literary scholars propose that the Koran in its original form no longer exists. There is no consistent opinion as to which autograph (reading) of the Koran is the original.

<u>Conclusion</u>

There has been little known textual criticism applied to the Koran. One main reason is the Koran's own statement that it is not to be doubted. This uneasiness and hesitancy in questioning the Koran precedes the rise of Islamic militancy. In the late 70's, John

[36] Hadith of Sahih Bukhari, Volume 6, Book 61, Number 510.

Wansbrough of the School of Oriental and African Studies in London pointed out that examining the Koran with "the instruments and techniques of biblical criticism is virtually unknown."[37] Alexander Stille details the violent threats and actions that have occurred against scholars who have studied Islam and the Koran subjectively. He quotes an unnamed university scholar: "Between fear and political correctness, it's not possible to say anything other than sugary nonsense about Islam."[38]

The New Testament text stands apart as the most copied and reproduced manuscript in history. They are been over 25,000 ancient manuscripts discovered with nearly 6,000 copies found in the original Greek text. This vast number surpasses any other ancient document including Julius Caesar's Gallic Wars or Homer's Iliad. Ravi Zacharias states, "In real terms, the New Testament is easily the best attested ancient writing in terms of the sheer number of documents, the time span between the event and the document, and the variety of documents available to sustain or contradict it. There is nothing in ancient manuscript evidence to match such textual availability and integrity."[39]

It is thus concluded that the main argument against the New Testament Canon, by which modern Muslims scholars seek to discredit the New Testament, is wholly invalid. Accepting the inspiration of the Koran over that of the New Testament would be similar to embracing Homer's Iliad as possessing a divinely originated theograph. The Muslim, in his earnest sincerity, may express many reasons why he rejects the Gospel of the New Testament, though literary criticism of the New Testament should not be one of them.

---

[37] Alexander Stille, "Scholars Are Quietly Offering New Theories of the Koran," *New York Times*, March 2, 2002, http://www.nytimes.com/2002/03/02/arts/scholars-are-quietly-offering-new-theories-of-the-koran.html (accessed November 26, 2009).
[38] Stille, "Scholars."
[39] Ravi Zacharias, *Can Man Live about God*? (Dallas: Word Publishing, 1994), 162.

Bibliography

Al-Bukhari, Muhammad Ibn Ismail. *Sahih Bukhari*, Volume 6, Book 61. Translated by M. Muhsin Khan. http://www.usc.edu/schools/college/crcc/engagement/resources/texts/muslim/hadith/bukhari/061.sbt.html (accessed August 12, 2010).

Clarke, W. K. Lowther, ed. *The First Epistle of Clement to the Corinthians*. London: Society for Promoting Christian Knowledge; New York: The Macmillan Company, 1937.

Crone, Patricia. "What do we actually know about Mohammed?" June 10, 2008. http://www.opendemocracy.net/faith-europe_islam/mohammed_3866.jsp (accessed November 27, 2009).

Epp, Eldon J. "Issues in New Testament Textual Criticism: Moving from the 19th Century to the 21st Century." In *Rethinking New Testament Textual Criticism*. Edited by David A. Black. Grand Rapids, MI: Baker, 2002.

Farid, Malik Ghulam, ed. *The Holy Qur'an: Arabic Text and English Translation with Commentary*. London: The London Mosque, 1981.

Geiger, Abraham. *Judaism and Islam*. Translated by F. M. Young (1896). http://www.answering-islam.org/Books/Geiger/Judaism/sec11.htm (accessed August 11, 2010).

Henry, Matthew. *Commentary of the Whole Bible*. Hendrickson, 2005.

Metzger, Bruce M. Quoted in Wegner, Paul D. *A Student's Guide to Textual Criticism of the Bible: Its History, Methods & Results.* Downers Grove, IL: InterVarsity, 2006. Originally from *Manuscripts of the Greek Bible: An Introduction to Greek Paleography*. New York: Oxford University Press, 1981.

Metzger, Bruce M. and Bart D. Ehrman. *The Text of the New Testament: Its Transmission, Corruption, and Restoration*, 4th ed. New York: Oxford University Press, 2005.

Stille, Alexander. "Scholars Are Quietly Offering New Theories of the Koran." New York Times, March 2, 2002. http://www.nytimes.com/2002/03/02/arts/ scholars-are-quietly-offering-new-theories-of-the-koran.html (accessed November 26, 2009).

Zacharias, Ravi. *Can Man Live about God?* Dallas: Word Publishing, 1994.

Paul Meets Mohammed: The Apostle and the Prophet

Seaport in Damascus, Syria

The quietness of the warm sunny afternoon was suddenly interrupted. Paul took his eyes from the crystal-clear heavens to view the small multitude of Arabic speaking men (with possible women – their faces were covered) strolling toward the port. His concentration returned to the sky. His eyes were not as sharp but he could still behold the glory of God in his beautiful firmament. Although now elevated in years, his desire to see Jesus part the sky in his coming still remained fervent.

Hearing the multitude of Arabic voices becoming louder, he turned to view the scene. As the crowd reached the port, Paul noticed that they all seemed to be surrounding one particular man. The man, probably in his late 50's, had a peculiar stoic but contented expression. In a moment the group was less than twenty feet away from Paul. The Apostle decided to walk the short distance down the north side of the port to escape the noise. After many years of beatings, scourging, and mob riots, it was now extremely difficult to bear the anxiety of large unknown crowds. (He considered the phobia as his thorn in the flesh). After escaping, he fixed his eyes again toward heaven and prayed, "*How long, O Lord*?" He smiled wearily. "*How long*?"

★ ★ ★

Mohammed was fatigued but encouraged. He was just returning to his home in Mecca with family for the first time in over five years. To his heart, an eternity had elapsed since the Quaryish had displaced him and his family based on his proclamation of Allah, the one true God, and his denunciation of the idolatry that plagued his country. Mecca, governed traditionally by the Quaryish tribesman, greeted the prophet's message with ridicule and reviling. But even with the resistance, it was the city of Taif that was Islam's greatest steppingstone. There, for seven days and seven nights, with fasting and prayer,

Mohammed spoke of the surrender (Islam) that was required by Allah. Upon the seventh night, more than two hundred men confessed openly that there was no God but Allah and, with Mohammed as his prophet. The prophet could only rejoice in the benevolence of his creator.

He needed a moment of serenity. Mohammed had learned early, as a young Hanif, that a believer should divide his life between the adoration of God, the contemplation of his own work, and the daily effort to assure his earthly existence. Even those in his innermost circle knew that their teacher was prone to separate himself for prayer while always remaining in visible sight. "Although I draw near to Allah," he had told them, "I still am available to you." Even with this invitation, it was silently known that no one was to disturb him during his times alone.

★ ★ ★

Paul heard footsteps of someone walking behind him. Turning his head, he saw that the middle aged Arabian was less than a stone's throw away. His eyes were now also attuned to the nearing overcast. Paul silently prayed, "*Is he one of thy elect, O Lord?*" His spirit became troubled as a deep abiding sadness overwhelmed his soul. "*What is it Lord?*" he asked immediately. After decades of enduring and suffering with and for the Savior, his own frail heart had become a deep ocean reflecting and mirroring the infinite heart of Christ. Before he could discern the inclination, he listened as the man spoke softly.

"The work of the sovereign Creator is most magnificent," Mohammed spoke in Arabic as his eyes continually looked heavenward.

Paul did not know whether the man was speaking to him or himself. But he knew the language of Arabic, so he decided to respond in agreement. "The heavens declare the glory of God; And the firmament shows His handiwork. Day unto day utters speech, And night unto night reveals knowledge." Paul looked to Mohammed and smiled before continuing. "There is no speech nor language where their voice is not heard."

Mohammed looked up in awe. The old man had slightly Jewish facial attributes, but his countenance beamed of a land much more distant. The most obvious traits of the elder besides his small frame and huge eyes were his scarred hands and head. The scarring on his head had healed long ago but the wounds on his hands, below the wrists, appeared new. The Arabian culture always prescribed that the younger kiss the hand of the elder after meeting. But with such an evident injury, even the knowledgeable Mohammed was hesitant to touch the stranger.

Paul sensed the man's hesitation. Having lived in Arabia for six years following his conversion, he knew the tradition well. Paul made a few steps toward Mohammed with his hand outstretched.

"Paul," he spoke gently. "Paul of Tarsus."

Mohammed took the hand and slowly brought it to his lips. As he released it, he wondered how such violent wounds could appear on so humble a man. Not wanting to pry too deeply he fixed his gaze back to the sky thinking about the psalm Paul had quoted.

"It seems you are familiar with two cultures," Mohammed spoke as he turned his head to meet Paul's eyes. "I am Mohammed of Mecca. Are you Jewish?"

"Yes," Paul replied stoically. "Circumcised the eighth day, of the stock of Israel, tribe of Benjamin, a Hebrew of Hebrews, and concerning the law...I was a Pharisee."

Mohammed looked deeper into Paul's eyes, attempting to read more into his words. The apostle spoke of his history with such meekness it was nearly impossible to detect whether he was proud or ashamed. Such discretion was a true sign of humility. Many of the Jews that Mohammed had encountered in the city of Yathrib possessed an aura of ethnic superiority. They had refused to acknowledge the spiritual possibilities of anyone besides themselves. He inquired internally considering the possibility that such a man as this might become a convert.

"You were a Pharisee?" Mohammed engaged.

Paul took a breath and smiled. "I was. But now what things were gain to me, these have I counted loss for Christ." When he noticed the Arabian beginning to concentrate upon his wounds, he spoke again. "I bear in my body the marks of the Lord Jesus Christ."

At this, Mohammed recognized who this man was. He pitied the aged fool. Had not this Paul known that there was only one Lord of the worlds, Allah, the Benevolent, the Merciful, and Owner of the Day of Judgment?

"I speak with the sincerest humility to you my elder," Mohammed spoke as he held his chin looking up at the overcast sky. "But does not your Torah, which I am very sure you know, proclaim one God and none besides him?"

"Without equivocation," Paul replied as he turned his body to the voice. He began to beckon with his hands. "One God and Father, God of Abraham, Isaac and Jacob, God and Father of our Lord Jesus Christ. He was born of the seed of David according to the flesh but declared to be the Son of God by the Spirit of holiness and power of his resurrection."

Mohammed became troubled by this camouflaged idolatry that Christians had so carelessly attempted to disguise as monotheism. How could this man being a Jew, possessing the knowledge of the one true God, ascribe to the sovereign Creator a partner - even a *son*? It was this spiritual transgression that, nearly twenty years prior, had caused him to withdraw from the traditional temple worship of Kaaba. The temple, believed to be built by Abraham, housed over twenty-five idol gods, believed to be the sons, daughters, and intercessors of the God of Abraham. It was at age twenty-five that he withdrew himself to be a Hanif and seek the true divinity. After fifteen years of meditation and seeking, he had received the first of his revelations from Allah's messenger Gabriel.

"I am an Arabian by descent," Mohammed spoke sternly. "A Muslim descendent of Abraham and Ishmael. I am also a prophet of Allah Most High." He sighed as he glanced at the incoming shallow waves. He then looked back to Paul. "It has been revealed that the Messiah came only as the Prophet of Allah. Worth and worship were not what he required for himself, but only for the one true Raab [Lord]. It was heresy of disobedient followers when they transgressed greatly by exalting him to deity and exaggerating a death that did not occur."

Paul looked steadfastly in the face of Mohammed. "I do not know of this God you call Allah," he spoke firmly. He then lifted his eyes to heaven as the sun peeked its rays through the clouds. "I believe in one God, The Father, the Almighty; Maker of heaven and the earth, of all that is seen and unseen. I believe in one Lord, Jesus Christ; the only Son of God, eternally begotten of the Father, God from God, light from light, true God from true God; he was begotten not made being one in essence with the Father. Through him all things were made. And for us men and for our salvation he came down from heaven: by the power of the Holy Spirit he was born of the Virgin Mary and became man."

Mohammed remained silent as Paul continued speaking as if the words were etched upon his heart.

"For our sake he was crucified under Pontius Pilate; he suffered and died, and was buried. But on the third day he rose again in fulfillment of the Scriptures; he ascended into heaven and is seated at the right hand of the Father. He will come again in glory to judge the living and the dead, and his kingdom will have no end."

"May I ask..." Mohammed spoke abruptly. If he were Jewish he would have rent his garment at the blasphemy just spoken. Paul's declaration sounded more to him like a Jewish philosophical fable than a true religion. He had heard traditional stories about the apostle's conversion, but he wanted to hear it for himself. "Did you receive this revelation from God or from man?"

He crossed his arms as he waited for Paul's response. The aged teacher crept slowly toward Mohammed while speaking.

"Dearest Mohammed, I make this known to you that the gospel I preach is not according to man, nor will it ever be according to man. Neither I received it of man, nor was I taught it, but it came to me by the revelation of Jesus Christ. I myself in times past thought I must do many things contrary to the name of Jesus Christ of Nazareth," Paul spoke, then sighed. The thought of his former life still troubled him to this day. "This I also did in Jerusalem," he continued. "Many of the saints I shut up in prison, having received authority from the chief priest; and when they were put to death, I cast my vote against them." The apostle dropped his head as he fought back tears. He could still see the faces of those who sung praises as they were being stoned, sawn asunder, and scourged to death. Gaining his composure he continued. "And I punished them often in every synagogue and forced them to blaspheme."

Mohammed too could see the tears welling in the eyes of the elder. Paul maintained his composure while finishing.

"While pursuing Christians even to the foreign cities, I journeyed to Damascus..."

Mohammed listened to the familiar Damascus Road conversion story. As he listened he discover how eerily similar Paul's experience was to his own. During a mountainous spiritual retreat in his 40th year, he had felt an overwhelming force, something like a shadow hanging over him. Unable to escape this force, he left the secluded mountain and ran across the path of Jabal an-Nur. This phenomenon of force became increasingly unbearable. After finding no escape, he sought death as the final refuge. He stood at the brink of a steep ravine seeking to end the fearful drama. As he readied himself to take that final step he heard the voice that saved his life.

"*Mohammed, you are the Prophet of Allah.*"

He raised his head to view the sky illuminated by a dazzling light. He turned again to see that the light was present on all sides. At that moment he fell down unconscious.

"At midday," Paul continued to speak. "Along the road I saw light from heaven, brighter than the sun, shining around me and those who journeyed with me. And when we had all fallen to the ground, I heard a voice speaking to me..."

After arising from his stupor of that vision, Mohammed had returned home. With much reluctance he felt compelled to go back out to his retreat. It was there at Ghar Hira that while asleep he became greatly disturbed in his subconscious. At that moment, before him, he saw a man dressed in white. The man approached him before speaking.

"Read."

"I don't know how to read," Mohammed replied, wishing to withdraw from the frightening voice.

"Read!"

"I don't know how to read," Mohammed replied again.

"Read," repeated the enlightened form. "Read in the name of your Lord who created man from a clot. Read, for your Lord is most generous. Who taught by the pen, who taught man what he knew not."

That was the first of many manifestations, and from that moment on, the illiterate Prophet had the impression that a book had been imprinted on his heart. It was now in his soul, that the knowledge of the one true and sovereign Creator, Allah, had brought the history of the prophets into final revelation.

"Why is it that you Jews are so prompt to idolize every image you perceive as a God or Lord?" Mohammed inquired of Paul. "Was it not enough that you Jews worshiped Baal, the brazen serpent, or the golden calf on Mount Sinai? It seems that the inherent plague of idolatry has become so prevalent that even a Pharisee can succumb to visions that promote such transgressions." Mohammed took a step back around Paul while keeping his head and eyes on his elder. "Why must you Christians promote an even greater sin by idolizing Jesus, son of Mary, who served God as a prophet and messenger? This man was a spirit of flesh and blood, created by God. The time has now come to believe in Allah and to cease teaching Trinity. This is better for you. Allah is only one God. It should not be conceived that in his transcendent majesty and holiness he has begotten or been begotten. Allah has not chosen any son, nor is there any along with him. Paul of Tarsus, I speak this to your shame!"

Paul remained silent as he knelt down to one knee. A warm breeze swept over him, and he could smell the fragrance from the ocean coming off the shore. He looked to the ground and saw a smooth white stone, which he picked up and held in the palm of his hand. He glanced at it before looking back to Mohammed. "*The stone which the builders rejected has become the chief cornerstone,*" he thought to himself. He kept the stone in his hand as he slowly rose to his feet.

"Who is this Allah?" Paul asked gently. "This is not the God of the Jews. The name of God was revealed to Abraham, Isaac and Jacob, and even Moses, as YAHWEH. I recall the name of this Allah during my time in Arabia," he stated as he walked near to Mohammed. "Is not this the name of the moon deity?"

Mohammed's outward humility hid his rising incensement. How dare this infidel so insult the Benevolent in the presence of his messenger?

"Allah is the true God of Abraham and Ishmael. I pose the question to you: Was it not promised that God would make a great nation of Ishmael and his seed?"

"Yes, but the promise..."

Mohammed vehemently continued.

"And is it not also true, from the words of your own Torah, that God was with child?"

"Yes, but..." Paul attempted to counter, becoming flustered by the rapidity of the Arabian's argument.

"Then why are you so surprised, my dear Paul?" Mohammed

spoke condescendingly as he gestured upward with his hands. "Why is it so difficult to realize that this great nation and presence of the everlasting God is with the people of Arabia in that God has established the true and final religion of Islam? This true surrender and worship was in place for centuries before your own people so grievously transgressed God's covenant with them. It has been left to us Muslims to procure the final revelation of God's will."

"I perceive that you believe the writings of the prophets?" Paul asked calmly.

"With strict absoluteness," Mohammed replied. "These are the messengers of Allah."

Paul mused. "Well if you believe their writings, have you forgotten the second Psalm where David spoke under the control the Holy Spirit saying, 'I will declare the decree the Lord has said to me, you are my son, today I have begotten you'?"

Mohammed grinned as he turned away from Paul. If it were not for his strict code of reverence for his elders, he would have laughed. He had heard the Hebrew and Greek Psalms. They were completely unreliable. It was obvious to most scholars that these books had been seriously altered to support Christian doctrine. He knew that in the years following the Jewish dispersion the text now referred to as the Old Testament had become completely spurious. There had been so many books added during the short reign of Judas Maccabeus, that any writing that claimed to bear the authorship of a patriarch was utterly fallible.

There were many other translations of the Scriptures. It was no shock to Mohammed that most of the translators were already followers of the erroneous Christian way. The tragedy was that these men would translate every passage with such a falsified bias. This Christian heresy was now based solely upon the foundation of those who willingly chose to create a false gospel rather than acknowledge the truth of Allah that Jesus Messiah himself had taught.

"These Psalms that you pronounce..." Mohammed exclaimed as he turned back around to face Paul. "They have been in the hands of so many wicked men that it is utterly impossible to accept any version that supports your Christian doctrine while opposing the knowledge of the one God." He looked into the sky. "Allah gave David the Psalms as a warning as he also spoke by the other prophets. By the hands of those who were greedy for gain, disciples of deceptions and prophets for profit, we now see the once glorious Psalms in a distorted fashion. It is transgression in this dispensation to adhere to any other religion besides Islam." Mohammed sighed deeply before looking back to Paul. He saw the white stone in his hand. "How shall Allah guide disbelievers after his message has come, bringing with it proofs of his sovereignty?"

Paul squared his shoulders as he looked into the deep penetrating eyes of Mohammed. He remembered the words he received from the Holy Spirit so long ago: "*Now in the last days, some will depart from the faith, giving heed to deceiving spirits and doctrines of demons, speaking lies and hypocrisies, having their own conscience seared with a hot iron; commanding to abstain from food which God created.*" It seemed to him that the fulfillment of the prophecy was standing directly in front of his face.

"If Allah is sovereign," Paul continued. "And if he is the true God of the Jews inspiring the words of the prophets, is it not possible for him to preserve his own words throughout generations? Is he not, as you say, owner of the heavens and the earth, able to do all things?"

"You know not what you mock!" Mohammed replied obviously disheveled as he walked toward Paul. As he walked the wind blew under his garment lifting up his skirt. For the first time Paul saw that Mohammed was brandishing a sword.

"You are correct," Paul stated confidently. "I am know not this God I mock." His nerves did not flinch one iota at the sight of the weapon. He was unafraid. He knew who he believed in, and was persuaded that Christ was able to keep him unto himself until that day.

All of a sudden, a young girl, accompanied by an older gentleman, came scurrying in their direction. Fixing her eyes on Mohammed, she separated from her companion and ran to him. With his mind still engulfed with Paul's blasphemy, he knelt down and hugged the child. She was a beautiful child with strong Asiatic features. She seemed to be eight to ten years old, with long brown hair and emerald green eyes. Paul assumed her to be one of Mohammed's children.

Paul smiled as he watched them converse joyfully. He himself had no children choosing rather to live a celibate life for Christ sake. His union of intimacy was that with Jesus, and through such a consummation, God had given him multitudes of children by the gospel of Christ. It was the church of God that was his offspring. No physical relationship could ever come near to such a bond.

Mohammed whispered to the child before kissing her on the cheek. She then walked past Paul without giving him the slightest glance before catching hands with her waiting companion. Mohammed made a gesture with his hand to the companion. Almost at once the man took a black cloth punctured with small holes from his sleeve. He then gently placed it over the head of the child. Her reluctance was obvious. The face of the child was now totally covered as she and the escort walked back to join the other company.

Paul silently prayed to God a prayer of thanksgiving. It was only by the love, mercy, and grace of God that he would bestow such wonderful gifts as lovely weather, food, and family, to men whom would so reject and oppose the truth of his Son. He smiled to Mohammed.

"You have a beautiful daughter," he stated as Mohammed looked to the party up the port. He looked back to Paul.

"She is not my daughter," he responded. "She is my wife."

Paul's heart became heavy.

"Please bear with me as my elder," Mohammed spoke humbly as he took a few steps towards Paul. "I share my testimony with the utmost humility. I was forced to leave my home in Mecca because I renounced the idolatry of Kaaba. This was because I announced my allegiance to the true God, your God and my God; the Most Benevolent. I and my family had to take flight because of the great persecution, humiliation, and failure that my message brought upon us. It was then that I and my fellow believers came to the city of Yatrhib and made a solemn treaty with the Jewish tribes present. They themselves were anticipating the advent of an Arabian Prophet. Even Jesus told his disciples that he would send a Comforter to bring them into the truth of Allah. I am the one to come after him. When they received me, I welcomed them into the faith as brothers. However, when they saw that they could not manipulate me for the dominion they were seeking, there arose resentment, plotting, and betrayal. Through a series of painful events, I and my followers were threatened with extinction. Violence was not what I ever desired, but when Allah spoke to me saying, '*that the persecution of his believers is a worse transgression than murder,*' I knew I had to act. I was again told, '*even though it is hateful for you Mohammed; warfare is ordained for you. Even the thing you hate.*'"

"With the treason of the Jews, an army of ten-thousand came against me and my fellow believers numbering barely two thousand men. I received from Allah the command to fight the persecutors. This was very distressing because of the fact that I have been a strict pacifist for thirteen years. It was then from Allah that we received the promise of victory. Against all odds, in the fiercest conditions, and after great opposition, it appeared as if we would soon meet our end. As we fought, however, something happened. The promised victory became ours. Our attackers fled from our presence. By the mercy of Allah, we won. And now..." Mohammed lifted his eyes toward heaven with his arms raised. "I trust that Allah will give us victory in the face of all our persecutors. The Muslims have taken over Mecca, and we shall continue to grow and expand."

Paul listened intently as only one emotion ran to his veins: pity. "*The end of this man is destruction,*" he thought to himself.

הו אלוהים, ירחם

"*O Lord, have mercy!*" He uttered in the Hebrew language.

"What was that?" Mohammed asked as he lowered his arms and fixed his eyes back to Paul smiling.

"It seems to me that your religion is one of might and force," Paul spoke humbly as he kneeled down and placed the white stone on the shore. "It also appears that this surrender, Islam as it is pronounced, is one phenomenon that does and continues to have violence as its linen and threading." Paul stood up. "In the Christian way, though we appear as men, we do not fight as men. The weapons of our warfare are not carnal..." Paul paused while again glancing at Mohammed's sheathed sword. "...but mighty in God for pulling down strongholds. It is through this might that we cast down arguments and every high place that exalts itself against the knowledge of God. The intention and action is to bring every motive, thought, and desire into captivity to the obedience of Christ."

Paul sighed

"Dearest Mohammed, if military conquest was an evidence of spiritual favor, how unjust would God be? For the wicked would be the most blessed, in this life and the next. No, but in the dispensation of times, God was pleased to confound the world by the foolishness of the cross. The Jews seek a sign, the Greeks desire wisdom, and you Arabs use force. But for those who know the truth, Christ crucified is the power of God and the wisdom of God. You see, God and his pleasure, has chosen the weak things of the world put the shame that which seemed so mighty. In this effect, no flesh can glory in God's sight. An omnipotent God does not need or desire force. He covets faith from a sincere heart."

Mohammed could no longer contain himself. He released a laugh.

"Faith in what?" he asked. "Faith in a mortal man named Jesus you Christians blasphemously deify? Is your God so weak, that he was terrified at the thought of death, praying that the cup of suffering might pass from him?"

"Though he was crucified in weakness," Paul replied, "Yet he lives by the power of God. For we also are weak in him, and we shall live with him by the power of God."

"And how can your God not even know the time of his own coming? Does this in itself reveal that he is not a knower of all things?" Mohammed asked.

Paul shook his head.

"The day of his coming is a day of wrath." Paul answered. "How could Christ know this wrath until the cup of anger was poured upon him from the Father? The eyes of the Father are too holy to look upon sin. Christ, who knew no sin, became sin for us that we might become the righteousness of God in him." Paul stepped forward before looking intently at Mohammed. "When Christ died for sin, he stood in the place of guilty men and women. You say that your God is merciful and forgiving, but where is the proof? Did not God tell Moses so long ago that it is the blood that makes atonement for the soul? If God had forgiven sin by a divine decree, or by some type of written declaration or recitation in book, or even by issuing some sort of celestial document written across the firmament - without the blood of Christ's cross, which involved the misery, suffering, and death of his only begotten Son - then we all could assume that God cared nothing of sin and the breaking of his law. Consequently we would go on sinning and the earth will become a living hell."

"Hell?" Mohammed responded vehemently as he paced the shore. He looked to the sky and saw the coming fog from the East. "There will be hell only for disbelievers of Allah, for those who reject his prophet and ascribe partners to the sovereign God of the universe. On the day of the resurrection, the angels will be a witness against you. Jesus the Messiah himself will testify against you, and the servants of Allah will drag infidels into the fire."

Mohammed turned around and walked back to Paul slowly. As he looked at him, he recalled the face of his uncle. Mohammed had pleaded with his dying kinsman to renounce the idolatry of Mecca and embrace the religion of Islam, but even unto death the man rebelled against the revelation. Mohammed's heart was pained to consider his uncle's future state.

Mohammed stepped directly in front of Paul. After staring into the cataract eyes he went into his sheath and pulled out his sword.

"*For me to live is Christ, and to die is gain,*" Paul thought to himself as he watched Mohammed hold the sword high. When the nearby entourage saw Mohammed's blade raised, they immediately freed their own swords and ran the twenty yards up shore toward the Prophet.

Paul silently prayed as he heard the thunder and saw the Mohammed's army racing toward him.

"*Father, I am ready to be poured out as a drink offering...*"

The army was quickly approaching, with weapons in hand. Paul closed his eyes.

"*And Lord,*" he continued as he saw a flash of lightning. "*If the time of my departure is at hand...*"

Those waiting for the ferry began to rush to the shore in expectation. The stampede became louder.

"*If my departure is at hand,*" Paul continued. "*I have fought the good fight, I have finished the race, I have kept the faith.*" He then opened his eyes. "*Oh Lord, my strength and my Redeemer.*"

Mohammed turned to his men and raised both of his arms. At this motion, they all instantly stopped. They stood around the two men and formed a circle, preventing the crowd from approaching the prophet. Paul could see that the tiny shore was now engulfed with Mohammed's companions, the Muslim women, shore workers, and townspeople. Mohammed looked at the crowd slowly before concentrating back to Paul.

"Thus saith Allah," Mohammed proclaimed in the hearing of all. "To all infidels, we warn you saying, 'If you do not believe, be warned of war against you from Allah and his messenger.'" Mohammed then bowed down to one knee and placed his sword at Paul's feet. At the teacher's ultimate gesture of humility, the entire army put away their swords. All eyes were on Paul. All of Mohammed's disciples knew that anyone their beloved master would make such obeisance to was worthy of prestige.

"The great Apostle Paul," Mohammed spoke in humble adoration.

Paul remained stoic as he listened.

"I know who you are and what you have done. I have listened to your epistles and heard of your life. And in many ways," the Arabian continued. "I have gained an enormous amount of inspiration from your endurance, your sufferings, and your zeal for the truth. I believe God has brought us together at a crossroads so to speak. This is the final bridge to cross: from a Jew, to a Christian, to a Muslim. It is the proper progression that Allah has prescribed for us."

Mohammed stood up and took Paul gently by the hand.

"Repent, Paul," the prophet spoke passionately. "You have a place with Allah and with us in paradise. Allah promises that he will love you and forgive you of your transgressions. Allah is forgiving and merciful. You may spend your years teaching and instructing with me, raising a family, taking wives."

Paul continued listening.

"Dearest Paul, believe me when I tell you this. In a few centuries after my departure, Islam will be the strongest religion in the Middle East. And soon after, by the power of Allah, we will be the strongest in the world."

At those words, the entourage of Mohammed broke out in shouting.

"Allahu-Akbar! (God is great)
Allahu-Akbar!
Allahu-Akbar!"

Once the shouting ceased Mohammed stretched out his hand again to Paul. "Now is the time," he proclaimed. "Will you join us?"

Paul looked at Mohammed. He loved him. Even with the venom of heresy that this man represented, he was still a soul created by God, for God, and would have no rest except in God. He was completely blind to the truth of Christ and was deceived by Satan himself. Paul then looked at the Arabian entourage. In the face of the twenty-five or so men and women, he could see millions who would lose their souls by choosing to reject the truth. And with his heart being a dim reflection of Christ, he could only imagine the pitiful torment that the Savior must feel. He wept.

"If I had rivers of waters in my eyes," Paul began to speak, "I could not cry enough tears for you and all those who choose to follow your way." His tears begin to flow as he released Mohammed's hand. All of a sudden the sun began to break through the overcast, beaming its rays upon the shore. Paul stretched out his arms wide and closed his eyes.

"I have been crucified with Christ," he uttered boldly for all to hear. He could feel the sun's warmth all around him. "Nevertheless I live. Yet it is not I who live, but Christ who lives in me. And the life that I now live in this frail body, I live by faith in the Son of God, who loved me and gave himself for me."

Paul opened his eyes before looking toward Mohammed. "God forbid that I should boast in anything except for the cross of Christ Jesus my Lord, by whom the world is crucified to me!"

Immediately one of the men from Mohammed's army unsheathed his sword and rushed toward Paul. Mohammed calmly stepped in the soldier's path.

"No," Mohammed spoke authoritatively. "Let Allah deal with him." Mohammed began to walk away as the others followed him.

As he walked, he stumbled on something in the sand. When he looked to see what it was, he noticed it was a small white stone. He kicked it to the side and walked away.

Appendix C
The Last Sinner

And below the hilt, in letters of gold, were written these words: "Whoso pulleth out this sword of this stone and anvil is rightwise King born of England." Though many tried for the Sword with all their strength, none could move the Sword, nor stir it. So, the miracle had not worked.

~The Sword in the Stone

The Post-Millennialists were right. The year was 2076, and the entire world had been evangelized for Christ. The lion had lain down with the lamb and the serpent was now a play-thing for children. Christ's kingdom had been established on earth. The only thing missing was Christ.

His name was Alexander Mantzios. He had witnessed his mother, father, two brothers, and an ex-fiancée come to faith in Christ. (She had ended their engagement only after he had refused to accept Christ for the 100th time.) The separation from her had been extremely difficult, but he knew that he could not form a marriage based on something he believed as a myth.

All nations upon earth took a spiritual census every year to determine who the remaining unbelievers were. Each able bodied person was to come to the designated city and sign The Confession of Life. If they received Christ as Lord, they were to sign on the right hand of the book. Those that did not believe were to sign on the left. The names on the left were immediately contacted by government officials. They had nothing to fear, except the plethora of ministers that would be sent to them for what they labeled, as a "Spiritual Debriefing." The traditional belief amongst the nations was that Christ himself would only return physically when every soul living was converted.

Alexander lay in his bed on a Saturday night and prepared himself to watch the news. It had been two weeks since the latest signing of the confession of life, and each year the list on the left would gradually decrease. The broadcast begin to report the new converts. With each new group of repenting sinners the nations would hold a festival in honor of grace. After that, theologians would commentate on biblical passages as they anticipated the days until the glorious appearing of Christ.

The report from the news anchor startled him. "*One non-Christian left on earth?*" Alexander jokingly thought that it must be himself. He had worked with many Christians in years past, but no real bond was ever formed. Even his mother and father seemed like distant strangers. He now spent most of his days fishing, drinking homemade wine, and playing with his dog Pathos. (He named him that because of a bad case of mange the dog had survived as a puppy.)

"*Alexander Mantzios, age 37, from Athens, Greece,*" the anchorwoman announced. He couldn't believe what he was hearing. At first he became frightened. Who knew if some fanatic might try to take his life in order to usher in this so-called second coming? His worry immediately subsided. There hadn't been a murder among the Christians in the last 50 years. But what he did expect was company. He knew that the nations would do all they could to convert the last sinner on earth.

★ ★ ★

The "C.C.N." (Coalition of Christian Nations), had held an immediate emergency conference on the island of Crete, even before the news report was broadcast. They needed to know everything possible about Mr. Mantzios in order that they might bring him to faith. Government background checks revealed that Mantzios had never claimed allegiance to any one faith. There was no record of baptism, confirmation, or any other spiritual ceremony related to his history. He was simply, and in every sense of the word, an unbeliever.

After much discussion and debate, Resolution 777 was declared. The resolution included the articles that the nation would monitor the whereabouts of Mr. Mantzios at all times to prevent him from going into hiding. Most importantly, the resolution included the declaration entitled, "The Final Debrief." This final debrief would include bringing the nation's top theologians, apologists, and evangelists to prove and persuade him to the faith. In the minds of the world's leaders, there was nothing more important than bringing this one man to Christ.

Alexander's phone had been ringing continually. Every time he answered, a zealous Christian would begin to explain to him the message of God's salvation. Some of the callers he knew, while others were complete strangers. Most were compassionate in their witnessing, but others were obtuse. After listening to the 50th caller he decided to take his satellite phone out of orbit.

When the world couldn't reach him by phone they came to his door. Neighbor after neighbor rung his alert tone, wanting nothing more than "*just a moment of his time*." The moments became unbearable, and after a while he stopped answering. He began to feel very claustrophobic as he realized that the interruptions and unsolicited guests would only continue coming.

To his relief, he was contacted by the Athens government. "Mr. Mantzios..." the Ambassador spoke to him the next day over his voicemail."We can only imagine all the disturbances you've been experiencing since the report came out. We would like to provide you a secure place to stay where your privacy will be respected." He accepted the offer, already knowing the catch. When he was escorted to the special location in Crete, he was informed that for six hours each weekday the nation's best ministers would speak to him at length concerning Christian doctrine. He was left alone in a nicely furnished living domain with a box of entrée supplies in the kitchen and a Gideon's Bible in a drawer.

The next three months on Crete passed very slowly. After 213 oral sermons, 96 in-depth Bible studies, and a massive amount of Christian literature bestowed upon them, Alexander remained an unbeliever. He was finding the Christian servants predictable, redundant, and rhetorical. He had considered lying numerous times and falsely proclaiming faith in this Christ. But he knew that it wouldn't suffice. If he lied, and the Man from Galilee did not appear, they would only intensify their oracles.

Alexander bargained the nations down to only witnessing three hours each day. He attempted to view the ministers as his daily source of entertainment for it seemed as if he could change the channel on the different types of homiletics he would encounter. There were the boisterous Baptists and the meticulous Methodists. There were the precise Presbyterians and the lethargic Lutherans. He wondered how and why the followers of this one Jesus had so many different names and approaches.

One of the most memorable ministers was a well-known Christian apologist name Hermann von Ludwig. He came from a long line of Presuppositional Apologists who were known for being able to convert anybody. He remembered the brief discussion all too well.

"Your reason for believing what you believe," Ludwig had said, "is based on reason, and your reasoning is circular. You first presuppose that what you believe is valid, but the criteria is based on circular reasoning. Your observation and logic for not believing do not support your naturalistic views. Therefore, your worldview is erroneous if it is based solely on your reason."

"So you're saying my reasoning is not valid?" Alexander asked after pausing for a moment to soak in all that the Apologist had said.

"Yes," Ludwig replied. "The reason of man is not a valid criteria for understanding truth."

"Oh's it's not you do say," he asked as he surmised the response of Ludwig. "My reason is not valid? Well I guess I have no reason to believe anything you say, seeing I have no basis of criteria for understanding it anyway."

Ludwig remained silent with a puzzled look on his face. That was the end of his argument.

"I presuppose this conversation is over," Alexander spoke in jest as his visitor left the room.

More months passed with more ministers. Alexander was astonished at the intellect of many of the men who came to visit him. He met with A.T. White, a doctor and leading theologian in the Anglican Faith. White had Ph.D.'s in linguistics, theology, and law. He was able to explain the Scriptures so profoundly and with such complexity that Alexander felt that he needed at least one doctoral degree himself to understand what was being said. After hearing some large words sounding like "Supralapsarianism" and "Homousia," he found himself dozing off.

The most peculiar ministry he encountered was a bunch known as Charismatics. This interesting group told him that he would believe instantly after they laid their hands on him. They even showed videos of their past revivals. It all seemed absurd to him, with people falling down on the floor and speaking in strange words. He decided to have fun with the group by faking the experience after they prayed over him. However, unable to contain himself, he finally broke out in laughter. When the men and women saw he was only joking, they called him everything but a child of God.

As more time passed, more ministers were sent. Yet despite the long lectures, sermons, and expositions, Christianity seemed to Alexander no more than a metaphysical fable with different interpretations. It did seem that there had to be some shadow of truth in Christianity, though, for the whole world had been evangelized, and no other religion had been able to do such. However, its followers seemed overzealous, preoccupied with their own agenda, or simply hypocritical. Here he had been on the island of Crete for almost an entire year, and his only guests had been the ministers who came to preach. He ate alone, took his walks alone, and did everything else alone. He silently wondered, "*If this man Jesus Christ was the personification of love, how come his followers couldn't be?*"

The burden of being the only so-called unbeliever was beginning to take a toll on his emotional and physical health. He was sleeping more and eating less. When he asked his host about seeing a doctor, he was told, "Friend, Jesus is the only doctor you need..."

He was tired of being preached to. He felt that he now knew more about Christianity than almost any Christian, and yet he still did not believe it. After arguing with the nations, they finally decided to discontinue their agreement to keep him in the secure place. This allowed him to leave the island. He knew that he would undoubtedly be monitored and pursued, but he believed that there had to be at least one place on earth where no Christian existed.

By the time he left the island of Crete, Alexander's face had become the most recognized in the world. News reports continually displayed his image with the caption: *The Last Sinner: Convert At All Costs*. The nations even offered a reward to anybody who would lead Alexander Mantzios to Christ. Alexander had hoped to find refuge with his parents in Italy, but when his mother and father discovered that it was their son who was the last sinner, they went on virtualvision and pleaded with the world to forgive them for having such a rebellious son.

In a last ditch attempt, Alexander made the mistake of trying to board a flight to the Gozo Islands, where he believed he could find some still feral lands on which to live in isolation. Hoping no one would recognize him, he grew a beard, dyed it black, and wore dark glasses. However, when his name was called over the baggage claim loudspeaker, he was mauled by over a hundred people pleading with him to believe in Jesus Christ. He tried to move away from the crowd, but they had him boxed in. It seemed as if each one of them was either putting a Gospel Tract in his face, or uttering Bible verses at him. He began to feel dizzy and flustered. The result was a panic attack that left him completely unconscious.

Waking up later that evening, Alexander found himself in the hospital. The cordial doctor detailed to him the diagnosis. "Well," the physician said with gentleness, "you have high blood pressure, you are malnourished, and you are suffering from anxiety. But I believe you've got an even bigger problem." The doctor sat down and pulled out a pocket Bible. "Have you ever heard John 3:16?"

Alexander thought to himself, "*Enough is enough.*" If he had felt strong enough, he would have immediately left the hospital. In his anger, he cursed the doctor with the pocket Bible and the nurse who brought him tracts every time she came to check his charts. He cursed the hospital that only allowed him to watch two movies: Lee Strobel's *A Case for Christ* and *Ben Hur*. But he stopped short of cursing God. He knew in his heart that God existed and that he was good. All he had to do was look at the wonderful things this God had made. It was Christianity that he was struggling with. It seemed that those who were now claiming to speak for God were neglecting the one thing he needed the most.

"I'm tired of hearing about Jesus!" he screamed as the nurse tried again to explain the Gospel of John.

"You deserve to go to hell," she lashed out in response.

"Good, I will gladly go to hell if I can get away from all you Christians!" he responded. The nurse left the room abruptly as he began to weep bitterly. Although many in the hospital heard him crying, no one came to his side. He felt so alone. He looked up to the ceiling and began to pray, "God, show me Jesus. Show him to me and I'll believe." After the tears finally stopped, he fell asleep.

When he was awakened by the nurse the next morning, Alexander was surprised to see a little blonde girl sitting in a chair toward the back of the room. He had never seen her before. She appeared to be around eight to ten years old. She smiled at him before lowering her heard to read her book.

"Who's the kid?" he asked the nurse coldly.

The nurse did not respond. She was one of the nurses he had cursed the night before, and since then she had spoken nothing but medical jargon to him. She wrote on her chart and quickly exited the room.

Alexander sat back in his bed and looked at the little girl again. He became suspicious when he saw that she was looking at a children's picture Bible. Who knew if someone was trying to use her to gain his compassion? He decided to simply ignore her and let her be. He would not fall into the trap of anyone manipulating his emotions. But to his bewilderment the girl remained quiet. She occasionally lifted up her head and smiled at him, but nothing more. It was a warm smile, and it did not appear that such a beautiful child could be coached into being the slightest bit comfortable around a total stranger. He could hear her quietly reading the words of the story, but he could not make out what she was saying. He tried his best to ignore her.

After about fifteen minutes of silence, Alexander began to grow agitated. "*Who was this girl, and how come she hadn't said anything?*" He thought it had to be a trick. He couldn't remain silent any longer.

"Well little girl," he finally spoke in her direction. She lifted her head as if waking from a sweet dream.

"Do you know who I am?"

She smiled as she nodded her head. "Yes, they say you're the last sinner." She stood up and began to walk toward his bed. He became uncomfortable.

"Well then, if you know who I am, aren't you going to try to tell me about Jesus too? Isn't that what you were sent for?"

"Maybe later," she replied in a soft melodic voice. "But for now, I just wanted to keep you company. I didn't want you to be alone."

The little girl then grasped his hand as she looked down at

him. It was the first time that someone had truly touched him in years. Alexander felt tears begin to well up in his eyes.

"Elizabeth," a nurse called out as she entered the room. "I've been looking all over for you. What are doing talking to him? Don't you know who he is?"

"Yes Mommy," the little girl replied. "I know, but Jesus loves him." She then held up the page of her picture Bible, which showed a bearded man in a white robe holding a heart-shaped world in his hands.

The nurse grabbed her daughter by the arm before speaking. "It's time for us to go now!" As the little girl was ushered out of the room, she turned and waved to Alexander, smiling. As he waved back, he noticed that the sensation of her hand holding his was still present with him. As the mother and daughter exited the room, he burst into tears. God had answered his prayer. Alexander now believed. And as he bowed his head in a prayer of thanksgiving, he could hear a trumpet sounding from a distance.

About the Author

Jomo K. Johnson is a licensed minister in the P.C.A. and current M.Div student at Westminster Theological Seminary. He holds a B.A. in Biblical Studies from Beacon University. He serves as Pastor of Philly Open Air Church Plant in Philadelphia and College Minister at New Life Glenside Presbyterian Church in Glenside, PA.

If you have any feedback or comments on this book, please email the author at: Jomo1980@aol.com. For more literature by the author, visit Phillyopenairchurch.com/Resources.html.

www.ingramcontent.com/pod-product-compliance
Ingram Content Group UK Ltd.
Pitfield, Milton Keynes, MK11 3LW, UK
UKHW020128250726
13967UKWH00002B/529

9 780557 579754